The SMiDGENS
CRASH-LAND

DAVID O'CONNELL

The SMIDGENS

CRASH-LAND

Illustrated by
SEB BURNETT

BLOOMSBURY
CHILDREN'S BOOKS

LONDON OXFORD NEW YORK NEW DELHI SYDNEY

BLOOMSBURY CHILDREN'S BOOKS
Bloomsbury Publishing Plc
50 Bedford Square, London WC1B 3DP, UK
29 Earlsfort Terrace, Dublin 2, Ireland

BLOOMSBURY, BLOOMSBURY CHILDREN'S BOOKS and the
Diana logo are trademarks of Bloomsbury Publishing Plc

First published in Great Britain in 2022 by Bloomsbury Publishing Plc

A catalogue record for this book is available from the British Library

ISBN: PB: 978-1-5266-4056-7; eBook: 978-1-5266-4054-3

2 4 6 8 10 9 7 5 3 1

Printed and bound in Great Britain by CPI Group (UK) Ltd,
Croydon CR0 4YY

MIX
Paper from
responsible sources
FSC® C171272

To find out more about our authors and books visit www.bloomsbury.com
and sign up for our newsletters

For my editor, Lucy Mackay-Sim –
thank you for everything!

1

Take-Off

Gafferty Sprout's parents had grounded her for a whole month after *The Incident*, as they called it. This was their way of describing what was, in fact, several incidents, where *incidents* was a polite word for *extremely-dangerous-and-insane-and-not-to-mention-totally-forbidden activities*. Activities which had put her family in danger and had nearly led to both Gafferty and her new best friend, Will, meeting their ends in a very horrible way. But that was ages ago – a whole month! – and now Gafferty was free. Free to have fun and free to have … more *incidents*.

'Does your dad know you're doing this?' said Will, as he stood by her side on the roof of the chocolate factory. He studied her face suspiciously. Gafferty's father was not someone to be crossed. Will sensed trouble behind his friend's mischievous grin.

'Don't worry,' she said, dodging the question. 'Look, I've been grounded for so long I just want to do something that is the complete opposite of being grounded. And you're going to help me: I want to fly.'

The breeze swept across her face as she looked out over the town below the factory. The human world was a place most Smidgens feared. But even though Gafferty was only seven centimetres tall (and that was when standing on tiptoe), for her it was the realm of adventure. She'd hunted chips in its takeaways, dug for treasures (useful, edible and ... otherwise) buried in its rubbish bins, and dodged the *kars* and *bysickals* that the silly Big Folk rode around its streets. It had given her new friends and presented her with strange and sometimes frightening experiences. Yes, it had been dangerous, but it had been totally worth it.

'I suppose the general idea of flying is to avoid the ground as much as possible,' Will conceded, as they strapped on their crash helmets. Gafferty had borrowed one of his spares. It had a bird's features painted on to it – all the Roost Clan dressed as flying creatures of one kind or another. 'But your dad says Smidgens were never

2

meant to fly. He won't like it.'

'We've done this before.' Gafferty grabbed the control bar of the training glider, copying the position of Will's hands. 'And you'll be right beside me the whole time. You're in charge – I can't go anywhere without you.'

Will nodded but still looked uncomfortable.

'We'll go on three,' he said reluctantly. 'One … two …'

'THREE!' shouted Gafferty, pushing them off the roof. Her stomach turned a somersault as the glider plunged unnervingly downwards, but at once she felt the smooth, strong force of the breeze passing over the top of its wings, the vibration travelling through the frame of the glider to her hands as the craft was lifted over the factory gates and into the sky.

'I'm in charge, you said!' yelled Will, fighting to get the glider under control, but Gafferty just laughed, filled with joy at the incredible sense of speed as the air rushed past her. They soared high over the houses of the Big Folk, leaving behind the grey-tiled roof of the factory which hid her home beneath its forgotten basement.

'Wheeeeeeee!' she said. 'The world is so BIG, Will! There's so much to explore! So much to do!'

'You've only just found out that your family aren't the only Smidgens left in the world,' said Will, as he banked the glider towards the centre of the town. 'You've united two of the old Smidgen clans who lost contact years ago, *and* seen off actual ghosts and evil Big Folk. Won't that do for now?'

'I suppose,' she grumbled, although when Will talked about *The Incident* like that it did sound rather impressive. 'But I've spent my whole life down in the Tangle. In those dark tunnels, running from place to place on our scavenging trips. You and the rest of the Roost Clan live in the daylight, Will. You get to see EVERYTHING from up here. It's so wonderful. I want to do more! I want to be free!'

She threw her arms out, letting go of the control bar so that she swung from the glider by her harness. The craft wobbled alarmingly.

'Let's just get to the Roost in one piece,' muttered Will. 'That will be a good start.'

'Wait! Look – the humans are having one of their markets!'

Gafferty pointed to the open square below. It was packed with food-laden stalls, their rectangular, stripy awnings forming a colourful patchwork, so the market resembled one of the quilts her mother sewed from scraps of stolen cloth. People were busy buying and selling vegetables, fruit and cheese, or chatting over the bread

4

and cakes and pastries. From so high above they didn't look big or dangerous at all. 'Let's get a better view, Will – please!'

Will rolled his eyes but tilted the glider so that it swooped across the marketplace. A couple of Big Folk glanced upwards but saw nothing but an odd-shaped pigeon darting overhead.

'That wheel of cheddar could feed us for ten years!' said Gafferty as they circled over a cheese stall. 'And those cakes – the smell of that bread! Will, we have to stop and grab some crumbs to take with us!'

'Gafferty – it's too risky! Don't be so silly.'

She ignored him. She knew it was silly. But all the colour and scent and noise – it was intoxicating! They were just the kind of experiences she wanted. She spotted a young human boy, standing next to a bakery stall, his hands reaching for a sandwich his mother had just bought him. He bit greedily into the deep filling of cheese and pickle. It looked very tasty.

FLUMPH! Gafferty was just aware of a flurry of feathers nearby when the glider was knocked forcefully sideways, wrenching their hands from the control bar. They spun violently, tumbling across the busy market and narrowly missing the clock tower that stood at its centre.

'A pigeon!' was all Will managed to say, as he fought to right the craft. Gafferty thought she glimpsed a bird's shape dart away across the square as they rolled with dizzying speed, the world cartwheeling around them. Whether it had bumped into them by accident or had seen them as a rival, the pigeon hadn't waited around to see the damage it had caused.

Will battled with the glider as Gafferty was flung about like a leaf in the wind. It dived back towards the sandwich stall, back towards the hungry boy.

'I can't keep us in the air,' Will yelled. 'We have to land!'

'We can't! The place is full of Big Folk!'

'It's too late!' Will gritted his teeth as they hurtled downwards. 'Hang on tight …'

2

Secret Agent Noah

The glider whipped over the heads of several unsuspecting humans, then plunged into the kiosk, landing heavily in the middle of a huge plastic tub of lettuce leaves. The impact sent the wet lettuce flying up around the Smidgens before it slumped back down over them like so many soggy bath towels.

For a moment, Gafferty didn't move, stunned by the collision. Then a huge drop of ice-cold water smacked down on to her head. It broke over her crash helmet, streaming freezing water over her shoulders. She let out a furious shriek. Will quickly hushed her.

'You're alive then,' he whispered, testing his arms and legs as he dangled from his harness next to her. 'That landing could have been a lot worse.'

Before Gafferty could think of an appropriately sarcastic response, he unbuckled himself from the glider and dropped into the salad leaves.

'We'll have to abandon the wings,' he said, scrambling over the sodden lettuce to the edge of the tub, 'and make for the nearest Tangle entrance. Do you know which one is closest?'

'No! I've not been through the market before.'

'What about your atlas? Can't that help?'

Of course! In her panic Gafferty had forgotten. Her atlas of the Tangle was one of her most prized possessions. Thankfully her scavenger bag had stayed dry. She dragged the book out and quickly flicked through its pages.

'There's one in the clock tower. It's not too far. But what about your glider? It's going to end up as the filling in someone's sandwich if we leave it.'

'It's too wet and heavy! And there's no time anyway! We'll be spotted any minute. Hurry up and let's move!'

They clambered up the slippery side of the tub and peered out from under the lettuce. Two huge brown eyes stared back at them.

'It was you! I thought I saw little people flying on that aeroplane thing,' boomed a voice. 'I didn't imagine it.'

It was the boy, his half-eaten cheese sandwich still in his hand. Gafferty guessed he was probably the same age as her little brother Gobkin. His freckled face was glowing with delight. 'Are you toys? I heard they were making action figures with artificial intelligence. Is that what you are?'

Gafferty glanced at Will, who clung to the tub's edge, frozen with fear. Big Folk children were dangerous: sharp-eyed, fast moving and unpredictable. There was no telling what they would do. But this boy didn't seem threatening.

Remember the Rules of the Smidgens, thought Gafferty, *the rules of survival*. Rule Four was: *if in doubt, make it up*. Gafferty had an uneasy relationship with Rule Four.

'You're absolutely right,' she said brightly, deciding to give it a go anyway. 'Arty-farty intelligence. That's us.'

'Arti*ficial* intelligence,' the boy replied doubtfully.

'Exactly. That's what I said.'

'You're very lifelike,' he observed warily. 'I expect that's an animatronic thingy. I've seen robot dinosaurs at a theme park. They were brilliant. Mum was scared but I wasn't. What's your name?'

'I'm …' Gafferty paused as she tried to think of a convincing name. 'I'm called Gafftimus Prime, and this is my friend Willbot Saladcrasher.'

Will narrowed his eyes at her but said nothing.

'I'm Noah,' said the boy. 'What kind of things can you do? Do you come with any guns?'

'I don't think so.'

'Oh.' Noah gave a disappointed sigh.

'Actually, we were just out on an exciting secret expedition from the toy shop, testing our glider, but we had a bit of a mishap with a pigeon. Terrible drivers, pigeons.' Gafferty slowly climbed out of the lettuce tub. She looked around. Noah's mother was busy chatting to the stallholder. No one but Noah had seen them. 'We'd better be on our way back or the shopkeeper will miss us,' she said. 'And it's best if you don't tell anyone about us. We might get into trouble. Or worse: sent back to the toy factory.'

'I can help,' Noah whispered. He grabbed a paper bag from a pile on the stall. 'Get in here and I can carry you a little way. I can't go far though.'

Will looked horrified at the idea. Gafferty hesitated for a moment. It was risky – very risky – but they were unlikely to get through the busy market without being seen otherwise.

'Just get us to the clock tower,' she said. 'Our computer brains will guide us the rest of the way.'

The boy nodded. Gafferty dragged the terrified Will into the bag.

'I'll put the rest of my sandwich in there with you, so it doesn't look suspicious,' said Noah. 'I can say I'm saving it for later.'

'You're good at this secret mission stuff,' said Gafferty.

'I'm going to be a secret agent when I grow up. Secret agents are always having to do this kind of thing.'

He gently picked up the bag and ran towards the tower before his mother could notice he was gone.

Cramped and uncomfortable, Gafferty and Will held on tightly to the sandwich as they were bounced around inside their paper hiding place, past all the unsuspecting shoppers.

'What is that smell?' said Will, covering his mouth. 'I think I'm going to be sick!'

'Don't you like pickle?' said Gafferty, nibbling on a breadcrumb. 'It is a bit on the spicy side.'

Fortunately, it wasn't long before the bag came to a halt and opened. They scurried out into the fresh air. Noah had been true to his word. Will's face flooded with relief when he saw that they were at the foot of the clock tower that loomed over the whole square. There was a crack in its ancient stone base, unnoticed by any Big Folk, but to any Smidgen it was obviously a door. Without stopping, Will dived straight through it to safety.

Gafferty, however, lingered. Noah had done them a kind favour, even though he believed they were hi-tech action figures. Would she have behaved the same if the tables were turned?

'Thank you!' she called up to him. 'I hope you get all the toys you want. With smarty-fish-hole intelligence and guns and everything.'

He grinned and waved.

'After all ...' Gafferty chuckled to herself as she dragged her scavenger bag through the Smidgen door. 'It's only fair after the amount of cheese I've just pinched from your sandwich.'

3

Crumpeck

Gafferty went back to Will's with him. She was excited to visit the Roost, nestled in the attic of the grand hotel, after her long month of being stuck indoors. And it didn't seem right that Will should get into trouble for losing the training glider on his own, as it was sort of her fault – *completely* her fault, according to Will – that they were flying through the market in the first place.

'We'd better not say anything about Noah,' said Gafferty. 'Talking to a human boy will get us into even more trouble.' Will nodded reluctantly.

The Sprouts' home, or the Hive as it had been known in olden times, was quiet and a little dull in comparison to the Roost, which was full of noise and colour when they arrived. Seeing the Roost Smidgens chattering away in their bird costumes was almost like watching a flock of sparrows squabbling over bread scraps. And their homes, which hung from the ceiling like nests, were, in Gafferty's opinion, completely adorable.

Will's older brother, Wyn, saw them clamber through the trapdoor in the floor of the attic, and ran over to greet them, smiling broadly as he recognised Gafferty. The smile left his face when he heard what had happened.

'Oh, Will!' He sighed. 'How many sets of wings have you lost or broken? You'd better tell old Strigida now and get it over with.'

Lady Strigida, the chief Elder of the Roost Clan, was standing before the enormous stained-glass window that let light into the attic space. The elderly lady was grandly bedecked in downy feathers and wore two amber jewels in her hair. They reflected the multicoloured spots of light from the window in a way that made them almost seem alive, staring at the children like the eyes of an owl.

'Gafferty Sprout,' Lady Strigida said sternly, as the trio approached her. 'The last time you came here you were a harbinger of misfortune. I hope your return is not prompted by further calamity.'

Nice to see you too, thought Gafferty, but before she

16

could say anything Will blurted out the whole story, or as much as they'd agreed to tell. Gafferty could see he was dying to confess about Noah. Lying didn't come naturally to him and he didn't like it.

'You've *lost* a training glider?' said Strigida after he had finished. 'You know we don't have many of those, Willoughby. What is your uncle going to say? And Gafferty, what does your father think about you flying through the Big Folk market? Does he approve of such perilous behaviour?'

'He doesn't exactly … know,' said Gafferty slowly.

Strigida rapped her paperclip walking stick on the wooden floor impatiently.

'The foolishness of youth!' she said. 'I know you are not a bad soul, Gafferty. Indeed, you are brave and passionate. But that can be a dangerous combination. You must learn responsibility.'

Gafferty was about to reply when she felt her scavenger bag trembling at her hip. She opened it and several lumps of cheese tumbled out, shaken free by the vibration.

'It's my knife,' Gafferty said. 'My glass knife is shaking. It's glowing strangely too. I wonder why.' She carefully took it out and with the touch of her hand the trembling stopped, and the glow faded.

'So, you keep it close,' Lady Strigida said quietly, eyeing the pink shard of crystal. 'Your piece of the Mirror of Trokanis.' Strigida had told Gafferty that if you looked into the legendary Mirror, you would be magically transported to any place you desired. It was like a doorway across space. The Mirror had broken long ago, during something called the Disaster. Gafferty didn't know much about it, but the Disaster was said to be so terrible it led to the Smidgen clans hiding themselves away from each other. Gafferty's troubles last month had really started when a human, Claudia Slymark, had come looking for pieces of the mirror along with her scary ghost servants. Gafferty's piece of the Mirror had protected her from Claudia's ghosts, but she wondered if they might come back for it one day.

'I'm keeping it safe,' she said. 'I promise. It never leaves my side.'

'Good. There's powerful magic in there, as you see.'

'I know. I'm being careful with it, really I am. I *can* be responsible.'

Strigida arched an eyebrow.

Before she could speak, there was a polite cough from someone behind them. Another Smidgen smiled meekly at their surprised faces, an older man with white hair and an untidy beard. His face had a jittery, wide-eyed expression, as if he were expecting someone to jump out at him at any moment. He clutched a bunch of scrolls to his chest.

'Crumpeck?' said Wyn. 'What do you want?'

'I'd like to meet Gafferty Sprout,' said the Smidgen. He eyed the knife in Gafferty's hand. It was a strange look, almost hungry. As he leaned in to study the knife more closely, a scroll toppled to the floor. He made a clumsy grab for it, sending all the other scrolls flying in every direction.

'I'm so sorry, everyone!' he squeaked, crawling on all fours after the escaping papers. 'I think I'm just a bit nervous at meeting the famous and brave child of the Hive.'

Gafferty laughed nervously as she quickly put the knife back in her bag. Famous and brave – *her*? But Crumpeck seemed quite serious.

'Gafferty Sprout, who dared the Tangle to find us,' he

continued, 'and unearthed a piece of the fabled Mirror. It's such an honour!'

'Erm … it's nice to meet you too,' she said, as she and Will helped the man gather up the strewn documents. The truth was she hadn't unearthed the knife, she'd merely picked it out of an old cat food tin her dad used for collecting discarded Smidgen tools – the knife had just been lying there. It did seem strange she had chosen it out of all the other objects. It was almost as if the knife had chosen her.

'Crumpeck shares my love of the Smidgen-lore,' said Lady Strigida, tolerantly. 'He calls himself a Smidgenologist! He will take over as the clan's keeper of knowledge when I am gone. He's been studying some manuscripts that I thought were lost but which he's recently rediscovered. And … well, he's made quite a breakthrough.'

'What kind of a breakthrough?' said Gafferty.

'I believe,' Crumpeck said, gripping the scrolls tightly, 'that after much research I have discovered the location of the Burrow – the home of the *third* clan of Smidgens! We've found them at last! After hundreds of years, all of the Smidgens can finally be reunited …'

4

An Expedition to Nowhere

Will and Gafferty glanced at each other excitedly. The Burrow! That meant even more Smidgens to get to know – and more friends.

'Tell them what you found,' said Strigida, prodding Crumpeck with her paperclip.

'It all started with Miss Sprout's book,' he began. 'The atlas.'

'That led me to Will and the Roost,' Gafferty said, 'but it only hinted at where the Burrow was.'

'A hint, yes, but it was enough. It pointed beyond the human town, to the Big Outside, and gave a general direction: north. I've been reading accounts of traders travelling from the Roost to the Burrow when there was still contact between the clans. This was centuries ago in the years just before the Disaster. None of the documents give proper instructions but some talk about routes or mention landmarks the traders passed. Some talk about the many days they travelled. Such tales!' He sighed wistfully. 'One even describes the Burrow itself. The clan made their home in a sandy bank, an old, empty warren of holes and tunnels that had been dug by rabbits. Putting all this information together has helped me build a bigger picture.' He grabbed a large, folded document from his collection of paper, sending the rest of the scrolls tumbling to the floor again. 'This is a new map of the town that I took from the reception desk of the hotel. And from all the accumulated information I've deduced that the Burrow is here.' His finger landed on a bare area, outside of the grey of the town. It was entirely green and had two strange words written on it.

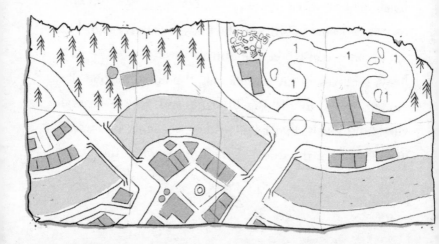

'*Golf course*,' read Will. 'What does that mean?'

'We don't know,' said Strigida. 'But we do know that there is a Big Folk bus that goes to it from the hotel. The humans travel there in the morning and the bus brings them back again later in the day. What they are doing at this place is a mystery, however.'

'Are we going to this golf course?' said Gafferty eagerly. 'Are we going to look for the Burrow?' It was another adventure! Her heart soared. But Strigida was frowning.

'*We are*, Gafferty,' the old lady said firmly. 'But I'm afraid I can't allow you to come with us.'

'Why not?' Gafferty's face fell. 'I found the Roost. It's me that's made this happen. Why shouldn't I go?'

'You're too hasty, Gafferty. Too reckless. This is something that requires careful planning and cool heads. Grown-up heads. Do we know the Burrow Clan *wants* to be found? What if they aren't pleased to see us? Smidgen has fought Smidgen in the past. Do we want to send our own friends and family into danger? It needs thought.'

'B-but—!' Gafferty stammered. Strigida raised her hand.

'I'm sorry,' she said. 'This latest incident with the glider has made up my mind. Your behaviour is too irresponsible.'

23

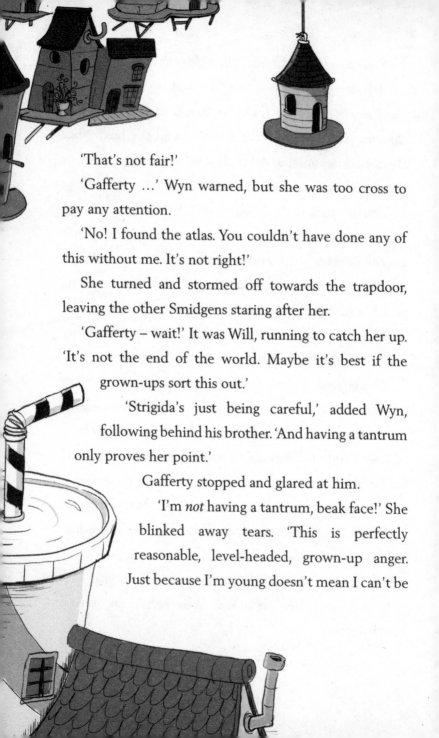

'That's not fair!'

'Gafferty ...' Wyn warned, but she was too cross to pay any attention.

'No! I found the atlas. You couldn't have done any of this without me. It's not right!'

She turned and stormed off towards the trapdoor, leaving the other Smidgens staring after her.

'Gafferty – wait!' It was Will, running to catch her up. 'It's not the end of the world. Maybe it's best if the grown-ups sort this out.'

'Strigida's just being careful,' added Wyn, following behind his brother. 'And having a tantrum only proves her point.'

Gafferty stopped and glared at him.

'I'm *not* having a tantrum, beak face!' She blinked away tears. 'This is perfectly reasonable, level-headed, grown-up anger. Just because I'm young doesn't mean I can't be

sensible.' She kicked at the floor. 'One minute everything's flying, the next we get knocked out of the sky. It seems to be a theme today.'

'You can't blame Strigida for wanting to keep her people safe!' said Wyn. 'It's her job. And you must admit, you've done some silly things lately. Your parents grounded you for a month!'

'They weren't silly things! And it all worked out in the end, didn't it? I united the two clans!'

Wyn suddenly exploded.

'You could have got my brother killed!' He was pale with fury. Gafferty had never seen him like this before. 'He only tried to help you, but he ended up putting his life on the line to rescue you from a mess that *you* created. I'm not going to let you do that again. We lost our mum and dad in a glider accident – Will doesn't remember, but I do. He's all I have left. And I'm not going to let some

daft girl take him away from me to die on another one of her ridiculous adventures!'

'Wyn!' his brother hissed at him, but it was too late. Gafferty's face was bright red.

'I would never, ever hurt Will!' Gafferty was almost yelling. 'How can you say that? I wish I'd never found the stupid Roost! I wish I'd never bothered looking for other Smidgens. I thought they'd all be nice and welcoming, and not like you and your idiotic feathery Elders.'

'And what about you and your family, running about dressed like bugs?' Wyn's face was so close to Gafferty's she could almost feel his contempt. 'I'm not surprised there aren't many of you left, with such obvious disguises! And the way you're going, you won't last much longer either!'

'I hate you!' she said. She turned away and ran for the trapdoor. 'No wonder my clan stopped talking to yours. It was because we realised you were a bunch of toffee-nosed, mean-mouthed squawk-bags! We're better off without you!'

'Gafferty!' called Will, his voice filled with anguish. Wyn caught his arm and held him back.

'I hate all of you!' Gafferty gulped through her sobs. 'I never want to see any of you again!'

She climbed through the door, tears streaming down her face and a sick feeling in the pit of her stomach. She could never go back to the Roost. After all she had been through, she was alone again.

5

Mr Ribbons

The thief gazed at the necklace, lying innocently in its carved wooden box. Diamonds glittered enticingly, inviting the touch of a hand. But the thief knew better. Claudia Slymark studied the gold chain links into which the jewels were set. There were markings, runes perhaps? She wasn't an expert in such things, but she knew a death curse when she saw it. Claudia carefully closed the box. This necklace was not to be touched, and definitely not to be worn, unless you planned on becoming a diamond-encrusted corpse. Either it would slowly tighten, strangling you before you knew what was happening, or the jewels were soaked in an invisible poison that would seep into your skin. Or they were actually the crystallised teeth of a vampire, poised to snap at your throat the moment you dared place the necklace anywhere in the vicinity of your flesh. Claudia had seen it all before.

Fortunately, she wasn't looking for jewellery for herself. This was a job for a client. She already had a necklace of her own, a chain of three glass bottles that clinked softly, the only sound she made as she worked. She placed the box in her bag, closed the safe she had broken open minutes before, and left the book-lined study, stealthily moving through the mansion's passageways. Her caution was the result of years of practice, even though she knew the owners were away.

'Another mission expertly executed, Miss Slymark,' whispered a cold, thin voice, leaking from one of the necklace bottles. Claudia ignored the compliment as she slid open the window through which she had entered the building earlier. 'Perhaps we could help on your next assignment?' the voice persisted. There was a detectable whine to its words, both pleading and resentful.

'And give you the chance to betray me again, Hinchsniff?' Claudia couldn't help herself, her normally cool demeanour overwhelmed by the heat of sudden anger.

'It wasn't me, it was Totherbligh!' the voice protested. 'It was his fault!'

'Trying to save your own skin, you feral nincompoop?' said a second voice. 'I was only—'

'Quiet!' snapped Claudia, zipping up her jacket and hiding the bottles from sight. The voice fell silent with a hiss. Claudia's wounds were still raw.

It was only a month since she had encountered the Smidgens, after being sent to their town by a mysterious client to discover the whereabouts of a magical object of which they supposedly had knowledge: the Mirror of Trokanis. It wasn't an unusual request, as stealing enchanted artefacts was Claudia's speciality. But the Smidgens, and a certain Gafferty Sprout in particular, had put up a fight, and Claudia had lost the one fragment of the Mirror she'd found – a tiny glass knife – just when it had almost been within her grasp. And, to make matters worse, the ghosts – her seekers, as she called them, who lived inside the glass bottles that hung at her neck – had even helped the wretched little people, fearful of the Mirror's powers. Perhaps it was understandable: one of them had been destroyed by the knife after all, and its bottle home was now empty. The other two bottles were still occupied but had remained tightly stoppered ever since. Claudia wasn't sure what she was going to do with her phantom servants.

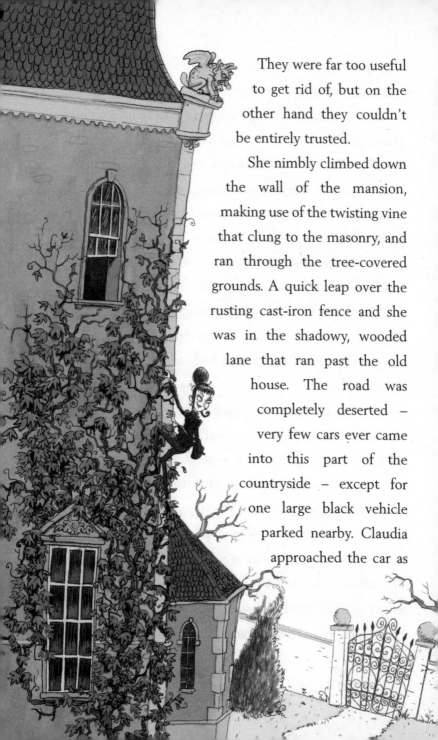

They were far too useful to get rid of, but on the other hand they couldn't be entirely trusted.

She nimbly climbed down the wall of the mansion, making use of the twisting vine that clung to the masonry, and ran through the tree-covered grounds. A quick leap over the rusting cast-iron fence and she was in the shadowy, wooded lane that ran past the old house. The road was completely deserted – very few cars ever came into this part of the countryside – except for one large black vehicle parked nearby. Claudia approached the car as its driver stepped out and faced her.

'You couldn't be any more conspicuous,' she said irritably. 'I mean, a hearse? I suppose I should be grateful that you're the only occupant.' She eyed the empty interior warily.

The undertaker was tall and completely bald, and looked very suited to his job. With his dark grey suit and square shoulders, he even resembled a gravestone. All he needed was *R.I.P.* written on his chest and you could plant him in a cemetery. Two tiny black eyes glared back at Claudia. She noticed the bottles had begun to quiver slightly under her jacket.

'You have the item?' he said, his voice like the creak of a coffin lid.

'Yes. Although I don't usually meet clients in person. It's too risky.' She handed him the box. He didn't even glance at it but continued to stare at her.

'It was a necessary ruse. The Mortiferum Necklace will be useful, I admit, particularly if trade is a little slow. Death is my business in more ways than one, you see. But hiring you to steal the necklace was the only way to meet you, Miss Slymark. I thought you might not agree to see me if I revealed my true intentions.'

The hairs rose on Claudia's neck. This wasn't a

33

collector. This was a magic user, some kind of witch or warlock, or a necromancer perhaps. She would have to be careful.

'What do you want?' she said.

'I believe you have another object of interest to me. Stolen from me, in fact, though so many, many years ago that I cannot blame you for that.' The man's eyes glinted hungrily.

'An object?'

'Three objects, to be precise. Though one of the three has been recently … emptied? I felt its passing, a disturbance in the ether – that is what brought me to you.'

Claudia drew a sharp breath but kept her face calm.

'The bottled souls you have,' the man continued. 'They are mine. My creation. And I want them back.'

The bottles trembled as if a fly were trapped inside each of them.

'I don't have them,' said Claudia, resisting the temptation to put her hand to her jacket to try and still them. 'You're mistaken. Now, I've completed the job so will be on my way if you don't mind.'

The man smiled. A black, lizard-like tongue flicked around his teeth.

'I see,' he said. 'I suppose a thief is bound to be unreliable when it comes to the truth. But I am prepared to be patient. It's something you learn when you are as old as I am. I will allow you time to reconsider.' From his coat pocket he produced a business card and handed it to her. 'Here are my details, should your attitude change. Do not think my patience is limitless, Miss Slymark. Nor should you make the mistake of thinking I am a fool. I shall be watching you.'

The man returned to the hearse. Claudia watched the car glide off down the lane, and realised she was shaking. She looked at the card. There was a name engraved on its velvety, skull-white surface.

Osiris Ribbons, Esq.
Servant of Death

6

Golf and Baked Carrot

The clang, clatter and clunk of machinery was louder than usual as Gafferty emerged from the Tangle via the storeroom mousehole. Although it was summer, the Big Folk of the chocolate factory were making lots of sweets in preparation for later in the year, for a time they called *Krissmuss*, which the Smidgens knew was some kind of eating festival. There would be plenty of pickings to be had for tiny hands and the Smidgens eagerly awaited *Krissmuss* as much as the Big Folk. Festive thoughts were far from Gafferty's mind, however.

More through habit than skill, she managed to avoid being seen by the busy humans and easily slipped into the basement where the Sprout home was hidden in a forgotten tunnel. In a daze she climbed the stairs of the rambling structure of the Hive on her way to the kitchen, Wyn's words still ringing in her ears. Her family were happily crowded around the kitchen table, about to sit down for their middle-meal: Mum and Dad, and her little brothers, Gobkin and Grub. Was Wyn right when he'd said they wouldn't last much longer? She couldn't imagine life without any of them – even Grub, sitting in his mother's arms, a psychopath in a slug onesie. Would he be the last of the Sprouts? He was starting to crawl, launching a reign of terror throughout the household. Nothing was safe from his greedy grasp. Gafferty had overheard Dad considering building a cage to keep him in, and she wasn't sure he was joking.

'There you are!' her father said accusingly, as she hugged him tightly. 'You couldn't wait to go off wandering could you, young miss? Out with your Roost friends, no doubt. I'm glad to see you're still wearing your spider-coat, at least, and not taken to beaks and plumes and Smidgen knows what else those odd folk wear.' When Gafferty didn't let go of him, his voice softened. 'What's this – tears? You sit down and tell your mum and dad what's happened.'

They sat in silence, eating the vegetable pie Dad had scavenged on a trip to the factory canteen, as Gafferty – having to stop every now and again to wipe her eyes and nose – described her argument with Wyn.

'Part of having friends is having ups and downs with them,' said Mum gently, after Gafferty had finished. 'You're bound to fall out now and then. You've got to learn to make it up afterwards. And you will go and say sorry, Gaf, after the things you've said.'

'But Wyn said horrible things about *me* – about us!'

'Out of fear. The lad probably puts on a show for his little brother, trying to look tough. But deep down, he's scared. He lost his parents, poor boy. He's scared of losing his brother too.'

'They said I was irresponsible. It's not true!'

Mum and Dad exchanged looks. Gafferty scowled.

'You're on their side, aren't you?' she said.

'You're a good girl,' said Dad, picking his words carefully. 'We're proud of you. But you've still plenty to learn, including knowing where your limits are. You test those limits, girl, because you've had to. Sometimes people are going to push back against you, and you must learn to accept it.'

'There are rules for surviving – you know that,' added

Mum. 'Well, there are also rules for surviving relationships with other folk. Only they're much more complicated and take longer to learn. And you can't go upsetting our neighbours like that, even if their ways are different. We need to respect them and their differences, and their opinions.'

'You wouldn't let me go on the expedition to the Burrow either, would you?'

'I'm certainly not allowing my daughter to go wandering into the Big Outside on the daft notion of some minion of Strigida's! I don't care if she's a Clan Lady or a Duchess of the Tangle, or the Grand High Smidgen herself.'

In other words, *no*. Gafferty sank into her chair. Mum and Dad didn't think she was responsible either, that was obvious.

'We need you here, Gaf, for now,' said Mum soothingly. 'We've run out of peppercorns and we're low on bark chips and a whole load of other things, so there's plenty of scavenging to keep you busy. And anyway, it sounds like they don't really know if the Burrow is at this golf course, whatever a golf course is.'

'It's a place where humans play golf,' piped up Gobkin, matter-of-factly. Although he was younger than Gafferty,

Gobkin was surprisingly knowledgeable about the Big Folk, as a result of his voracious reading habits. His main source of information was *The Big Book of Big Folk Facts*. 'It's a type of sport.'

'A *sport*?' said Gafferty.

'Humans play games with each other, like we do. But grown-up humans are embarrassed about playing games. They think they're something for children, so they call their games *sports* instead, and make up lots of complicated rules about how to play them. They argue and fight over the rules, which they seem to enjoy so much that some sports are just fighting and aren't really games at all.'

'Does golf have lots of fighting?' said Gafferty. She imagined the golf course to be a terrible noisy battlefield, filled with battered and bruised humans blundering furiously around.

'I don't think so,' said Gobkin slowly. 'Although they do have to use clubs. But not for hitting each other. They try and hit balls into holes in the ground that are a long way away.'

'What in Smidgen's name for?' Mum laughed. 'Why don't they just walk over and drop the ball into the hole? They must miss all the time.'

'And if you've got spare holes lying around, why not

do something useful, like plant trees in them?' added Dad.

'What happens if the ball goes in the hole?' Gafferty said.

'Nothing,' said Gob. 'That's it, I think. Big Folk are very strange.'

No one could disagree with that. The family continued their meal in silent contemplation at the weirdness of humans, except for Grub, who made handprints on the table using some baked carrot he had thrown up earlier.

That night, Gafferty lay wide awake in the wall nook where her bed was. How had this day gone so wrong? She couldn't bear it if Will and the others thought badly of her. And she couldn't bear the fact that she might be missing out on the expedition to the Burrow because of it.

In the dark she reached underneath her pillow and touched the cold glass of the knife. Once, she had heard voices coming from it, as if it were speaking to her. She had a connection to the knife, and she wanted to know how, and why.

'I bet there are more pieces of the Mirror at the Burrow,' she said to herself. 'The Burrow Clan might have the answers I need. But if no one lets me go there, how will I ever find out?'

7

Glass Magic

By the time she arrived back at her London apartment, Claudia was also feeling increasingly uneasy. She wasn't used to this: she was normally confident and self-reliant, sure in the knowledge that she *never* made mistakes. It had been the key to her success and was the reason why this apartment was one of several she owned all over the world. Stealing magical objects was lucrative because it was difficult. Claudia had a talent for sailing through difficulties. But at this moment she felt like she had run aground. First, the Smidgens, and now the menacing Osiris Ribbons.

Without changing from her working clothes, she sank into the luxuriously padded armchair in her study. She removed the bottles from her neck and placed them in a row on the desk in front of her. They had been silent and still since the encounter with the undertaker, unlike their usual chatty selves. They had never spoken about their past and Claudia had never questioned them – she hadn't been particularly interested, if she was honest – but it was time she got some answers.

'Talk,' she said. 'Tell me everything.'

Shapes moved restlessly inside the glass containers. They were clearly agitated.

'Please don't give us back to him, Miss Slymark!' spluttered Totherbligh, his bottle rocking backwards and forwards in distress. 'He's pure evil!'

'Then tell me what I want to know. He said he was your creator. Is that true?'

'He was our *gaoler*!' snarled Hinchsniff. 'A wicked man, he conjured our spirits from their graves and bound us to these wretched prisons.'

'Why? And why *you*? What makes you special?'

'In life, we were his servants,' whimpered Totherbligh. 'He is a necromancer – he commands the dead to carry out his wishes. But he had living helpers too. Through the years, each of us served the cursed villain in turn.'

'Some of us were more useful than others,' muttered Hinchsniff.

Totherbligh ignored him.

'Ribbons's magic meant he outlived us, but for us death was no release from his control. Instead, he continued to make use of our spirits. It was an act of cruel treachery after all our years of thankless hard work.'

'He should have left us in peace,' put in Hinchsniff. 'Unlike you, Miss Slymark, he has no principles whatsoever. He'd hurt us with his magic if we didn't do as he asked.'

'And the bottles?' asked Claudia.

'Ghosts aren't normally mobile – their hauntings are tied to a place or a thing,' explained Totherbligh. 'A grave, perhaps, or the scene of a violent death. Ribbons bonded us to magic-infused glass to allow him to take us with him on his travels.'

Claudia sat up suddenly.

'Magic-infused glass?' she said slowly. This sounded very familiar …

'Not glass, exactly – crystal. The bottles are carved from gemstones and jewels. They gain their powers from the magic of the earth, and some are even born from the fire of dragons, the stories would have you believe.'

Claudia raised an eyebrow but said nothing. Her mind was working busily.

'Ribbons upset someone important,' Totherbligh continued. 'I don't know what happened – I think he raised someone's granny from the dead and she turned up at their house for lunch half decomposed, or something like that. Anyway, he disappeared for a while. His property was confiscated by the authorities and placed in that bank vault where you found us with the other magical relics. He must have been furious. The bottles were hard to come by, and extremely valuable.'

'And that's why he wants them back,' said Hinchsniff miserably. 'Corpses, the undead, phantoms – they're two a penny for Osiris Ribbons. It's not *us* he's after. It's the bottles.'

Claudia lounged thoughtfully in the armchair. She didn't like being told what to do, especially by creepy, corpse-bothering old men. The ghosts might be a bit unpredictable, even duplicitous, but they were useful, and besides, they were hers by right. Everyone knew that finders were keepers – it was the foundation of thievery, an agreed principle of the criminal underworld. Osiris Ribbons was breaking the rules. However, the threat of returning the ghosts to Ribbons would help to keep them on a leash if they misbehaved again.

The undertaker would have to be dealt with somehow. He was dangerous, but perhaps he would be open to the idea of a bargain … He was after magical glass and she knew where to find some: the Mirror of Trokanis. Plus, she had an empty bottle which she might as well let him have, as it was no good to her. That should keep him happy. And as for the client who was seeking the Mirror … well, they would never find out. It was quite possible the pieces were lost for good after all.

There was another reason Claudia wanted to continue her search for the Mirror, one that lurked in a dark place at the back of her mind. She didn't like to admit to such feelings. Feelings were a nuisance in general. They were distracting, unprofessional. But whenever she thought about the Mirror, she thought about Gafferty Sprout. And the thought of Gafferty Sprout – the tiny girl with the big mouth, the wretched Smidgen who had humiliated her – made Claudia's blood boil. Claudia wanted revenge.

The ghosts had gone quiet again, so she put them in a drawer of the desk and flicked through the pile of letters she had picked up from her mailbox on the way in. She immediately spotted the distinctive handwriting on one of the envelopes, the odd, forced letters pressed into the paper as if the writer had struggled to hold the pen. The letter was from the mysterious client who was searching for the Mirror – had they been reading her thoughts? She'd not been in communication with them since she had failed to take the knife from Gafferty, as she'd been too ashamed to admit her defeat. She hurriedly opened the envelope, nervous fingers tearing at the paper.

The message was short and simple, but for the second time that day, Claudia was left with a cold, unpleasant feeling of dread:

WE NEED TO MEET.

8

A Surprise in the Cupboard

'Gobkin, did you pack the strawberry jelly slices?' asked Gafferty, looking up at him from her scavenger bag and scratching her head.

'Yes.' Gobkin sighed, sitting impatiently at the kitchen table. He tapped the top of his rucksack, all fastened and ready for their trip. 'I already said so. It seems like an awful waste if you ask me. We should be eating jelly, not wearing it.'

'There's plenty of jelly in the factory for both eating and for our sticky shoes. We use the old dried-up jelly that no one wants to eat.'

Gobkin frowned. Gafferty had caught him having a crafty nibble from one of the slices when he thought no

49

one was looking, and he obviously disagreed.

'If there's some left over you can have it,' she said with a grin. 'But don't tell Mum and Dad.'

She did another check of her own kit: pin hooks, fishing line, thread, a pot with a damp square of cloth in it, and, of course, her glass knife. If her brother started complaining, there was some food to keep him quiet, sealed inside a screw-top container their mother had recently scavenged. Mum had said a human used it to store the little pieces of transparent plastic that they put on to their eyes to help them see. She called it a *Len's Case*. Gafferty didn't know who Len was, but a Smidgen could use the lid as a plate, so the case worked perfectly as a picnic basket.

Realising she'd forgotten the match-head torches, Gafferty ran to the storeroom to fetch a bundle from inside the fireproof tin in which they were stockpiled.

'Come on, you muddle-head,' she scolded herself, as she grabbed a piece of sandpaper to light the torches. 'Pay attention!'

She was trying hard to be a good example to her brother, teaching him the family's scavenging methods, but her thoughts kept creeping back to the argument of the day before. She wasn't looking forward to facing Will and the others again, but Mum and Dad said she had to apologise. She also couldn't stop thinking about Crumpeck's discovery. An expedition would be so much more exciting than the trip they were about to take.

Dad had asked them to go to the factory cleaners' cupboard to fetch a wash cloth that could be cut up to make a fresh supply of nappies for Grub. They were in high demand. How could the little squirt, well, *squirt* so much poop from his rear end? What on earth was he eating to make such a mess?

'We're ready,' she said, returning to the kitchen with the match heads and trying to put the thought of Grub's toilet habits out of her mind. Dad poked his head from behind the workshop door to give them some last directions before they departed.

'This should be an easy hunt for you two,' he said, eyeing them both sternly. 'The cleaners only come in the evening so there shouldn't be a need for any Big Folk to be in the cupboard. Grab the cloth and help each other to roll it up like a rug, and bring it back home, quick as you can. And don't forget the Rules.'

They nodded and hugged him briefly before disappearing down the stairs and out of the Hive. It didn't take them long to reach the cleaners' cupboard in the storeroom, as all the factory workers had stopped for lunch, so the place was deserted.

'Is it time for a snack yet?' asked Gobkin, as they stood before the cupboard's towering metal doors. 'I ought to keep up my strength.'

'Not yet, you ravenous bellymonster! Don't forget we'll have middle-meal when we're back home. Mum's baked lemon cakes – you'll need to leave room for those.'

'Perhaps I could have a nibble of jelly,' Gob suggested.

'Definitely not,' Gafferty said firmly. 'We're going to use that in a minute.'

A corner at the bottom of one of the metal doors had bent slightly, leaving a gap the two young Smidgens could slip through. Gafferty dragged a match head against her sandpaper scrap, its flash of powerful light illuminating the insides of the cupboard. It contained several mops in buckets, along with bottles of cleaning chemicals on its floor. High over their heads were a set of shelves stacked with dusters and cloths. It would be a long climb to get to their goal, so their sticky shoes would come in handy.

Gafferty produced the pot with the damp cloth in it, and some long pieces of thread. She laid the thread on the floor and Gobkin reluctantly placed two slabs of jelly on top of the thread and put one foot on each slab,

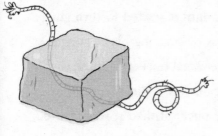

① Lay thread on floor
and
place jelly slab on top

② Place foot on to slab
and
tie it on with thread

③ Rub underside of jelly
with damp cloth until
it is 'GOOEY'

④ Press foot against
wall to test stickiness

tying the thread round his feet so that his boots were newly soled with strawberry jelly. Gafferty did the same. Then she rubbed the underside of each dried-up jelly slice with the damp cloth, until it started to turn gooey. Gobkin tested the tackiness by pressing his boot against the side of the nearest large metal bucket. It stuck with a satisfying squelch. Gafferty threw a pin-hook line over the rim of the bucket, and once satisfied it was secured, she pulled herself up the side, walking up the surface using her sticky shoes.

'See?' she called down to Gobkin. 'The stickiness helps steady the climb and saves your arms a lot of effort.'

'We should use those Upliners that Will and his friends have,' said Gobkin, referring to the mechanical winches that the Roost Smidgens used. 'Then we could use all the jelly for eating.' He wasn't wrong about the Upliners, Gafferty had to admit, but the reminder of Will and the Roost just brought back memories of the argument. The more time passed, the more stupid the whole thing seemed. Gafferty's foot slipped momentarily, and she dangled from the bucket like a spider spinning its web. She would have kicked herself were her feet not covered in jelly. *Concentrate, Gafferty! You'll be no use to Gob if you fall and break your head.*

'Are you OK?' called Gobkin.

'Yes,' she said irritably, clambering the last few centimetres to the top of the bucket. When she was sitting astride its edge, she helped pull Gobkin up after her. Then they shuffled on their bottoms along the bucket's rim until they reached the wooden handle of a mop that had been propped inside it. Using their pin hooks and sticky shoes they hauled themselves up the long handle all the way to the first shelf with its pile of blue-and-white-checked cloths. They took a minute to catch their breath.

'These Big Folk cleaners aren't very tidy,' Gobkin remarked, as he pulled the jelly from his boots. 'Look, the cloths are all scrunched up. It's like something's made a nest in here.'

Gobkin was right, it did look like a nest. Then Gafferty heard a scuffling noise and the cloth pile twitched – there was something in there! She froze. Was it a mouse? Or worse – a *rat*? She grabbed Gobkin's shoulders and put her finger to her lips, backing them slowly away from the rustling material. Whatever was in there, it was waking up! They scurried towards the mop handle and had just reached the edge of the shelf when the pile unfolded, and a sleepy face emerged from between the sheets.

'Oh, hello,' it said, blinking at them. 'Any chance of some breakfast?'

'Crumpeck!' gasped Gafferty. 'What are you doing here?'

'Looking for you, Miss Sprout,' the man said, crawling awkwardly from his makeshift bed. 'Although I confess, I seem to have taken a wrong turn.'

'And you're late,' said Gobkin. 'Breakfast was hours ago.'

'But ... what do you want me for?' said Gafferty, still astonished. 'What's going on?'

'I'm on a very important mission, Miss Sprout,' said the Smidgen, lowering his voice. 'A mission of the greatest daring and the utmost secrecy ...'

9

The Secret Embassy

Gafferty dropped her bag and ran forward to help Crumpeck as he shakily got to his feet.

'You don't look like someone who's on a daring mission,' observed Gobkin, as the Smidgen stretched and rubbed his neck sleepily. Crumpeck was dressed in his bird clothes, but his grey coat was patched and had a few sad, scruffy feathers stuck to it, and on his head was a pointed cap that was faded and crumpled. In all, he resembled a pigeon that had perhaps fallen down a drainpipe or barely escaped with its life from the claws of a cat.

'Appearances can be deceptive, young man,' said Crumpeck, smoothing his coat down. 'It's all part of the subterfuge, you know.'

'What subterfuge?' said Gafferty. 'Crumpeck, tell us what's going on. You half scared us to death just then.'

The Smidgen cleared his throat.

'I do apologise to you both,' he began. 'You see …' He paused and looked around him, as if there were hidden ears listening. 'I'm going to the Burrow!'

Gafferty didn't know what to think. How could this be true?

'But Lady Strigida said any expedition needed careful consideration. And that was only yesterday.'

'Of course, she has to say that *publicly*,' Crumpeck replied, with an attempt at a sly wink, 'as she's our leader and she has to be seen to be wise and far-sighted. But really, she's as keen as you or me to head out on an adventure. So, she's sent me – unbeknownst to everyone at the Roost – on a secret mission to make first contact with the Burrow Clan.'

'*You?*' Gafferty said, her face screwing up in disbelief. How could Strigida say Gafferty was irresponsible, and then send Crumpeck out instead? He might be an adult, but his appearance didn't exactly shout 'courageous explorer'.

'Well, yes, actually.' Crumpeck looked slightly deflated

at her response. 'I may not look like an adventurer, but I am utterly fearless at heart, I can assure you.'

There was a sudden metallic clank behind him and Crumpeck leaped in the air with a shriek.

'What was that?' he said, spinning around, his eyes wide in terror. 'Squirrels? Owls? Snakes? Owlsnakes?'

'It was me,' said Gobkin, looking guilty. 'Sorry, my snack seems to have dropped out of Gafferty's bag by accident.' He picked up Len's Case from where it had fallen as Gafferty glared at him. 'I thought your friend might be hungry,' he added, shrugging.

The man eagerly took the plate from the boy and gobbled down the spicy potato Mum had supplied as Gobkin watched enviously.

'Look, Crumpeck,' Gafferty said, speaking more gently. 'Are you sure that's what Strigida wanted? After all, you've told us about your secret mission, so it's not very secret now, and you've managed to get yourself shut in a cupboard. I'm fairly certain the Burrow isn't here. So, it doesn't seem like you've had a lot of success so far.'

'A few missteps, that's all, Miss Sprout,' Crumpeck said between mouthfuls. 'I made an unfortunate miscalculation when flying through the factory last night – I've never had much of a head for heights,

59

I'm afraid – and ended up with a bit of a bumpy landing on the top of this cabinet. While climbing down I was shut inside by the Big Folk and had to spend the night here. If only I'd known there was another way out! But it was very dark, of course. However, the fact that you've chanced upon me is confirmation of your destiny.'

'My what?' said Gafferty. 'What are you talking about?'

'You must come with me, of course!' Crumpeck dropped the plate and clasped her by the shoulders. 'Join me on this secret embassy to the Burrow. You set the Smidgens on this historic path, Miss Sprout, and you

60

should lead us on the next stage of this momentous journey. Your name will go down in the annals of Smidgen history as Gafferty Sprout, the Great Uniter of the Clans. Just think of the adventures! Think of the discoveries!'

He stared at her delightedly. For a moment she couldn't help grinning back. A chance to go the Burrow! It was exactly what Gafferty had been hoping for – an opportunity to get answers about the knife, to find more Smidgens. She would show Wyn and Strigida that she could be responsible, she would prove them wrong!

So why was she hesitating? She knew that she was sometimes impulsive, but she wasn't stupid. And there was something about what he was saying that didn't ring true.

'Did Lady Strigida actually ask you to take me?' said Gafferty.

'Not … exactly,' said Crumpeck. 'But she'll come round to the idea, I'm sure. And you want to go on this expedition – you said so yourself.'

'Yes, I do. I *really* do.' Adventurous Gafferty was battling Responsible Gafferty. She looked at her brother. She had to do the right thing. 'But I've got to get Gobkin home in one piece, and that's no small matter. And I can't just leave without saying goodbye to my parents. Why don't you come back to the Hive and we can talk about it? Make a proper plan.'

A look of anger briefly flashed across Crumpeck's face.

'I see that you doubt me. I am not a Smidgen-child, Miss Sprout. I know what I'm doing. If you're not going to come with me now, then I will be on my way before anyone finds ou— That is, before I waste any more time.'

He picked up her bag from where it lay, dropped the plate back into it and handed it to her.

'Thank you for the food. I have a copy of your atlas with me so can quite safely continue my journey through the Tangle. On. My. Own.'

Without another word, he grabbed a small rucksack from under the cloths and scampered to the mop handle, shinning down it to the bucket.

'Crumpeck – wait!' Gafferty called, but he didn't look back. They heard a crash and an 'Ouch!' as he tumbled to the bottom of the cupboard, and then hobbling footsteps as he staggered out through the gap in the door and into the factory.

'That was weird,' said Gobkin, as they peered over the edge of the shelf after him. 'He was desperate for you to go with him, and then suddenly he dashes off as if he can't wait to leave.'

'I hope he'll be OK,' said Gafferty, biting her lip doubtfully. 'He might actually be the one Smidgen more accident-prone than Will.'

'He seems to be a few crumbs short of a biscuit if you ask me.' The boy tapped his head with a finger. 'Maybe Strigida was hoping he wouldn't come back.'

'That's what worries me.' Gafferty sighed. 'I don't think Strigida – or anyone – knows what he's up to at all …'

10

The Betrayal

When the two young Smidgens returned home, carrying the rolled-up blue-and-white cloth upon their shoulders, they were surprised to find a breathless Will in the kitchen with Mum and Dad.

'Lady Strigida told me to come and tell you the news!' he was saying, as Gafferty and Gobkin stowed away the cloth in the workshop. He ignored Gafferty, keeping his serious face fixed on Dad. 'It's Crumpeck – he's disappeared! He vanished in the night and no one's seen him since. If you see him in the Tangle, Strigida wants to know about it.'

Gafferty and Gobkin exchanged a look.

'We've seen him,' said Gafferty, and recounted their

meeting with the Smidgenologist in the cupboard.

'Strigida will be furious when she hears this,' said Will. 'There's no way she would have sent him on any secret mission. She would have got into trouble with the other Elders if she'd done that. Roost Smidgens can't do whatever they feel like.'

Gafferty winced. That was directed at her. Will was still upset.

'He sounds like a proper bundle of bother, this Crumpeck fellow,' said Mum, eyeing them both as she prepared the middle-meal at the table. 'Our Grub causes less chaos, and that's saying something.'

'I think he's become obsessed with finding the Burrow,' said Will, looking uncomfortable. 'His house is full of old books and writings about it. And the Mirror of Trokanis too. Lady Strigida says he can't stop talking about it, and how wonderful it would be if he found all the pieces.'

'No, it wouldn't,' muttered Mum, chopping a raisin into chunks so vigorously the table wobbled. 'Magic is best left behind in the past where it belongs.'

'I wonder if that's why he wants to find the Burrow,' Will continued. 'Not because he wants the clans to reunite, but because he wants to put the Mirror back together.'

'Well, he won't while I've still got a piece of it safe in here,' said Gafferty, digging her hand into her scavenger bag. Her face fell.

'What is it?' said Dad.

'It's gone!' Gafferty emptied her bag on to the table, scrabbling amongst her scattered kit for the glass knife. 'It's not here! I know I packed it this morning!'

'You did,' put in Gobkin. 'I saw you do it. And I saw the knife in there when Len's Case fell out of your bag when you were talking to Crumpeck.'

Gafferty's eyes widened as the horrible truth dawned.

'He stole it!' she gasped. 'Don't you remember, Gob? He put Len's Case back in my bag – he must have slipped the knife into his coat then without me seeing!'

'That's why he was so keen to leave, all of a sudden,' said Gobkin. 'He'd got what he wanted.'

'How could I have been so stupid?' Gafferty was furious. 'He didn't really want me with him on the expedition after all. He just came here so he could get to the knife!'

'Are you sure?' said Mum.

'We would have heard the knife if it had been dropped somewhere,' Gob pointed out. 'And he was acting very oddly.'

'I know he did it.' Gafferty's face was set in a grim expression. 'There was a look in his eyes when he saw the knife yesterday. It reminded me of someone, but I couldn't think who at the time. Now I know: Claudia Slymark. It was a greedy look.' She jumped up from her chair and threw her kit back into the bag. 'I'm going after him.'

'You are not.' Dad rapped his fist on the table. 'If Crumpeck is this deceitful, it makes him dangerous, in my book. You will stay right here.'

'Dad, I have to go,' Gafferty said. 'I promised to take care of the knife exactly because it was so precious. It was my responsibility, and now that I've lost it, it's my responsibility to get it back. You want people to take me seriously, don't you?'

She glanced at Will, who stared at his feet. Dad bit his lip and stayed silent. Mum wasn't so easily put off.

'You don't even know where Crumpeck's gone,' she said. 'And he's got a head start on you.'

'His glider is damaged, so he's using the Tangle,' said Gafferty, slinging the bag on to her shoulder, 'and no one knows the Tangle like I do, and no one's as quick as I am – not even Dad – and especially not a bumblefoot like Crumpeck. And I think I know where he's heading.'

Will's face lit up for the first time.

'The bus for the golf course!' he said. 'That's how the Big Folk go there. He's going to try and hitch a ride.'

Gafferty nodded. 'I reckon I could easily catch up with him before he gets to the bus stop.'

'Don't go on your own, Gafferty.' It was Dad talking, quietly but firmly. 'Take Will with you. And don't do anything foolish. Follow Crumpeck but leave him be. It's too risky. If he gets to the bus before you, then let him go and come straight home.'

Will looked briefly at Gafferty. She gave him a weak smile and he nodded.

Gafferty hugged her father quickly and the two Smidgens headed for the door. Mum ran after them with a paper bag of raisin chunks and lemon cakes.

'You've not even had your middle-meal,' she said anxiously, tucking it into Will's rucksack. She blew them a

kiss and they set off, running as fast as they could into the Tangle.

They dashed through the tunnels, Gafferty's quick feet leading the way as Will plodded determinedly behind. They ran in an awkward silence, neither wanting to be the first to speak. Gafferty occasionally checked the atlas she always carried, looking for a shortcut or a route that might cut off Crumpeck's path. However, she needn't have worried. As the tunnel entered a large badger-dug cave, Will grabbed her arm and pointed to a distant figure, scrambling slowly along over the loose earth and stones on the far side of the hollow. There was no mistaking the scruffy old Smidgen, wisps of feather falling from his coat as he stumbled clumsily towards the cave's exit.

'It's Crumpeck!' Gafferty whispered. 'We've caught him! Now I'll teach that thief a lesson.'

11

A Dangerous Detour

'Your dad said we shouldn't tackle him, just follow where he goes,' hissed Will as they crept through the old badger sett.

'We're not in any danger,' said Gafferty confidently. 'Crumpeck's harmless.'

'You don't know that!' Will snapped. 'Whatever's got into him, it's making him do daft things.'

'Fine,' she sighed. 'Just keep up, will you?' Gafferty had no intention of leaving Crumpeck alone but this wasn't the place for another argument.

They steadily gained on the Smidgenologist. He appeared to be tiring, his walk slow and shuffling. *Perhaps he's having doubts*, thought Gafferty. *Perhaps he's realising he's done something stupid*. Either way, they would easily catch up with him at this rate.

Suddenly he stopped and stretched. Gafferty instantly froze and Will piled into the back of her, sending her flying into the dirt with an undignified squeak. Crumpeck spun around and gave a yelp at the sight of them. With renewed energy he sped out of the cave and darted down a narrow tunnel that forked off from the main path.

'You clumsy featherhead!' muttered Gafferty as Will dragged her to her feet.

'I couldn't help it!' he snapped back.

'We almost had him. Where is he going now? That isn't the way to the bus stop.'

'He could be trying to lose us,' Will said as they gave chase, following Crumpeck into the side tunnel. It was dark and winding, and they quickly lost sight of him, but there were no doorways or exits, so they knew he must be somewhere ahead.

Eventually the path stopped underneath a roof of wooden boards. One board had an opening cut into it, a Smidgen-sized porthole that allowed daylight to shine faintly into the tunnel. Cautiously they pulled themselves through the little window and found themselves in a narrow gap between a wall and an enormous white structure that towered towards the ceiling of a human-sized room. The machine hummed with electricity.

'It's a *frij*,' said Will. 'We're in the kitchen of a Big Folk house. This could be really dangerous.'

Gafferty bit her lip. This wasn't good news. Smidgen expeditions tended to stick to shops or cafés or factories, places where Big Folk behaved predictably, places they went with a purpose. Their homes were another matter: you couldn't know where the occupants of a human house might be at any time, and it had the added risks of the Three Great Perils, according to *The Big Book of Big Folk Facts*: cats, the terrifying *vakyoomkleeners*, and most fearsome of all, the type of human child known as a *todla*.

They edged along the back of the refrigerator. Clearly, no one had cleaned behind it in years as they had to kick through the dust, peas and other food scraps that lay there slowly fossilising. When they reached its corner, they peeked out across the expanse of the kitchen floor. A set of tiny grubby footprints weaved their way over the patterned tiles to the door on the other side of the room. Apart from the hum of the fridge it was quiet.

'Hopefully nobody's home,' said Will.

Gafferty nodded, then suddenly gave a sharp intake of breath. She pointed at one corner of the kitchen where

72

two plastic bowls sat on the floor.

'A pet!' said Will, horrified. 'What if it's a cat? This is way too risky, Gafferty. We have to go back.'

'No, we don't. Just keep your eyes open. We'll be fine.'

'You're not listening – this is too dangerous.'

'I am listening. But we've got to do this, or we lose Crumpeck and the knife. There isn't time to think or go and have a lovely chat about it with your Elders, Will.'

'This is typical of you, Gafferty. Wyn's right—'

Gafferty didn't wait to hear what Wyn was right about. She remembered his words well enough, and they still stung. She hated sniping at Will, hated getting him into trouble, but she was still angry at him and right now chasing Crumpeck was the only thing stopping her from shouting at him.

Following Crumpeck's tracks, she sprinted to the door. It was shut, but there was a big enough gap underneath for her to slide through without too much difficulty. She faced a carpeted hall that ended in the front door of the house and had two further doorways leading off it. Crumpeck's footprints ended here: the carpet was made from thick, twisted green wool that she had to wade through like a field of knee-high bristly grass. She heard Will puffing and panting as he scrambled under the door behind her.

'So, you decided to follow me anyway?' she said.

'Crumpeck's from my clan. This affects me too. Did he go out into the street?'

'I think he's hiding somewhere, the sneaky sneakface.'

There were voices. Human voices, from upstairs. There were Big Folk at home!

'We're leaving in half an hour.' It was a woman. 'Could you keep an eye on your little sister while I quickly tidy up downstairs? I don't want your Auntie Carol thinking we live in a pigsty.'

There was a muffled reply, then the sound of footsteps rapidly coming down the stairs.

'We need to hide – now!' cried Will. Gafferty grabbed his hand and dragged him across the carpet and through one of the doorways. They entered a living room, the furniture centred around a large TV screen that the Big Folk seemed unable to live without. Toys were littered over the floor: cars, plastic bricks and balls, and a selection of stuffed animals. There was a pile of drawing paper and some crayons. The woman was right – it was a mess, but that meant there were a lot of hiding places. They dived behind a pile of colourful wooden blocks that had been roughly stacked to make a wall.

The woman passed through the hallway to the kitchen without stopping. They could hear her in the kitchen, busily stacking dishes. They were safe for the moment.

'What are we going to do?' said Will, gasping for breath.

'Give me time to think! And stop making that growling noise – it's really distracting me.'

'I'm not making any growling noise.'

'Then … who is?'

They peeped over the wall. They weren't alone. There was Crumpeck, crouching in the corner of the room, his back braced against the skirting board, his face a picture of terror. He was trapped, his way out blocked by two large paws. As still as a statue – except for its tail, which twitched irritably from side to side – and keenly eyeing the little man in front of it, sat an enormous ginger cat. And it was not in a good mood.

12

Let's Go Digging!

'We have to get that thing away from Crumpeck!' said Gafferty. 'Distract it, somehow.'

Will gulped. 'How are we going to do that without it coming after us? We're the perfect size for a snack.'

'I don't think it's hungry, otherwise it would have eaten Crumpeck already. And then I'd only get my knife back when it ... came out of the other end. And I'm certainly not waiting around for that.'

She glanced around the room. Among the abandoned toys was something that didn't quite belong. It was a toy mouse, one that had seen better days. Its fur was all ripped, its felt tail had been chewed, and it had an eye missing. That kind of damage hadn't been done by a child – it was a toy meant for a cat.

'Rule Four,' said Gafferty, gritting her teeth, 'it looks like it's time to let you out of the cage once more …'

Before Will could stop her, she jumped up from their hiding place and ran over to the mouse. The cat didn't notice, its eyes fixed intently on the cowering Crumpeck. It appeared to be deciding what kind of game it would play with its little prisoner. Gafferty tied the ragged tail of the mouse around her waist and started running towards the huge animal, lugging the toy after her. The mouse bounced across the carpet as she ran, as if it had suddenly come alive. Gafferty crept up behind the cat, getting as close as she dared. She waited for the twitching tail to pass over her head, then THWACK! She jumped up and hit the tail with the palm of her tiny hand. It wasn't enough to hurt the animal, but it was enough to get its attention.

As soon as she saw the cat's head spin around, Gafferty ran as fast as she could in the opposite direction, heading back towards the wall of blocks. The mouse jiggled in her wake, its movement irresistible to the cat, which leaped to its feet. Crumpeck seized his chance and began to crawl away – but he moved too soon and too slowly. The cat saw him trying to escape. With a quick swipe from its giant paw, it knocked him over and pinned him to the floor. The mouse was a familiar toy to the cat; Gafferty realised the animal was far more interested in its odd new plaything and the strange, terrified squeaking noises it was making. Rule Four had failed her!

'Have you completely lost your marbles?' said Will, as Gafferty rejoined him behind the wall, the mouse still tied to her middle. 'You could have been eaten trying to rescue Crumpeck!' Gafferty wasn't sure, but there seemed to be a hint of admiration in his voice. 'What are you going to do now?'

'I don't know!' she said crossly. 'I'm always the one who has to come up with a plan. Why don't you think of something for a change?'

Will bit his lip. She could see he was trying. Then his eyes lit up.

'I've an idea,' he said. He pointed to a battered toy truck, a yellow loader with large black wheels and a big spade-like scoop on its front. For some reason it also had wobbly eyes and a smiling face. 'That thing can drive by itself,' Will explained. 'I've seen them in the toy shop. You press a button on the back that switches on some machinery inside that makes them go.'

Gafferty shivered at the thought of the smiling machine coming alive.

'You want us to dig our way out of here?'

'Don't be silly. But I think the cat will pay a bit more attention to this than a tatty, one-eyed mouse.'

It was worth a try. They scampered over to the truck. Will quickly found the button that started it.

'There's a little wheel on the top to make the big wheels point in the right direction,' he said. Gafferty clambered up to the cabin. The steering wheel was meant for small human hands but Gafferty could move it easily enough.

'Ready!' she called.

Will flicked the switch. The truck stirred into life, whirring and buzzing. Two orange lights on top of the cabin flashed.

'*Let's go digging!*' said the truck cheerily. Gafferty almost fell off her perch in surprise.

'It's talking!' she hissed at Will, as the truck moved forward. 'Is there a ghost trapped inside it?'

'No! It's just a bit of the machinery doing that,' Will said. 'Big Folk love this kind of thing. Watch where you're steering!' He chased after the truck and jumped aboard as it began to trundle across the carpet.

'*Let's go digging!*' the truck trilled.

Gafferty turned the wheel and aimed it straight for the cat's hairy behind. The animal's ears flicked around at the noise and it turned on the loader, its back arching warily. It let out a growl. Crumpeck lay motionless on the floor. Gafferty hoped he'd only fainted, and that it wasn't anything worse.

'Let's go digging!' The truck steadily advanced.

'I wish it would stop saying that!' said Gafferty. 'Come on, you stupid cat! Move out of the way!'

The cat raised itself up, hissing and spitting, and backing itself towards the wall, as the loader's scoop edged towards it.

'This thing's making a lot of noise for a toy,' said Will, having to raise his voice about the engine sounds. 'It's even making the floor vibrate.'

Before Gafferty could answer, the cat suddenly sprang away from the wall, jumping clear over the truck. The Smidgens ducked down as the furry monster's body sailed overhead and darted out of the room.

'That was close!' Gafferty shouted. 'But it worked! It's hard to believe a cat would be scared of a silly talking toy.'

'*Let's go digging!*' the truck said brightly.

'It's not!' Will shouted back. 'That noise, the vibration – it's not the truck making it! Look!'

Behind them, nosing through the doorway, was another machine, huge and animal-like but with no friendly smile to be seen, just a wide expanse of a mouth sweeping across the floor. The human woman was pushing it back and forth across the carpet, as it whined and roared. Dust whirled around inside its clear plastic drum like a churning thundercloud.

'That's what the cat was afraid of,' yelled Will. 'A *vakyoomkleener*!'

Gafferty gasped. They'd escaped one of the Three Great Perils by being rescued by another! She and Will jumped from the truck before they were seen. The loader trundled on its way into the wall where it stuck fast, its wheels turning helplessly as it pushed against the skirting board.

Gafferty and Will picked themselves up and raced the last few steps to where the cat had left Crumpeck. He was breathing!

'Help me get him under the sofa!' said Gafferty. 'We can hide there.'

They hauled the little man by his arms towards the darkness under the seat. He was heavier than he looked. The roaring of the *vakyoomkleener* grew louder and the floor trembled around them.

'It's coming this way!' yelled Will. The machine glided menacingly along the edge of the sofa, moving nearer and nearer. Air rushed past them, sending dust and clumps of cat hair spinning and tumbling before they were swiftly drawn into the *vakyoomkleener*'s mouth.

'Get back, Will!' shouted Gafferty, hauling him further into the darkness.

'But Crumpeck!' Will gasped. Gafferty realised that the older Smidgen's legs were still sticking out from under the sofa. He was right in the *vakyoomkleener*'s path! Before either she or Will could do anything, Crumpeck's body was caught – dragged towards the machine by its powerful suction. The *vakyoomkleener* engulfed him and, in an instant, the Smidgen was swallowed whole.

13

Surprises

'Stop!' cried Will, running towards the monstrous machine. 'Stop! You have to stop!'

'What are you doing?' Gafferty grabbed him by the shoulder before he got to the edge of the sofa. 'You'll put us all in danger!'

'It's you!' said Will, angrily shrugging off her hand. 'This is your fault! You're the one who puts us in danger!'

At that moment, the *vakyoomkleener* came to a halt, its motor whining into silence. Had the human heard Will?

'Could you come and clear up these toys of Rosie's for me, love?' the woman called. 'I need to get ready for work, and Auntie Carol will be here soon.'

She was talking to the person upstairs. Then she walked out of the room, leaving the *vakyoomkleener* behind. Ignoring Will, Gafferty peered out from their hiding place. Thankfully, there was no sign of the cat. Next to the sofa, high above her head, she spotted Crumpeck inside the *vakyoomkleener*'s dust chamber. He looked like he'd been dragged through a hedge backwards, forwards and sideways, but he was still in one piece. And he was moving!

'He's all right, Will! Crumpeck's OK! We can rescue him.'

'How?' Will folded his arms sullenly.

'We can climb up the side of the sofa and get to that dirt bucket thing from there. There must be a button or something that opens it.'

Without waiting for him to answer, she pulled her rope and pin hooks from her bag and threw a line that caught in the fabric of one of the seat cushions. She hauled herself up on to the sofa. The now mute *vakyoomkleener* stood nearby but was still too far to reach.

'It's you!'

A voice: one that Gafferty recognised. She turned to the doorway. There was a human boy standing there staring at her.

'It's you!' she said. She could hardly believe it. 'Noah from the market!'

'What's going on?' said Noah. He loomed over her. She tried to look calm but readied herself to run. 'What are you up to?'

'We're just on another outing from the toy shop,' Gafferty said, as matter-of-factly as she could. 'Exercising the smarty-squish-ball intelligence.'

'*Artificial* intelligence,' said the boy, frowning. 'I'm not fooled, you know. I went to the toy shop and the shopkeeper didn't know anything about you. You're not toys, are you? Toys wouldn't steal cheese from my sandwich.'

Gafferty's mouth flapped open and shut as she desperately tried to think of a believable explanation, one that would allow them to escape. Rule Four had let her down last time she used it. It was time for something even more desperate: the truth.

'You're right,' she began. 'We're not toys, we're real people. Just little – or at least, little compared to you. We're called Smidgens and … well, we need your help. Again.'

'I knew it!' he said. 'There was something odd about you. Little people! Are there lots of you? Do you live in the house? I bet you're the reason behind things going missing, like when I can't find my marker pens, even though I know I put them in the cupboard. That's you, isn't it?'

'No.' Gafferty sighed. 'That's you being forgetful. We pinch a bit of food, or things no one wants any more. We don't take things from kids. Apart from the occasional piece of cheese.'

'You seem to get into trouble a lot, whoever you are.'

'Yes, we do!' It was Will, shouting up from under the sofa. Gafferty could just see his cross face peeking out. His anger had made him fearless. 'Gafferty's always getting us into trouble.'

'I can't be bothered to argue with you now, Will,' she shouted back. 'We've got more important things to think about. Noah, could you help us get our friend? He's got a bit stuck.' She pointed at the *vakyoomkleener*. Crumpeck was staring at them from the dust-filled drum, his hands pressed up against the transparent plastic.

Noah raised an eyebrow but immediately unclipped the container. He gently tipped it on its side, allowing Crumpeck to slide out on to the sofa. The Smidgenologist was covered in so much cat hair he resembled a dishevelled rat.

'I *hate* cats,' was all he said. He coughed and spat out a ball of fuzz.

'You've no right to complain,' snapped Gafferty, 'after all the upset you've caused. We're taking you home now, whether you like it or not. Hopefully the return journey won't be quite so tricky.'

'That reminds me,' said Noah. 'I've got something for you. I'll be back in a minute. Just keep an eye on Rosie for me.'

He disappeared out of the room.

'Who's Rosie?' said Gafferty.

'Her!' said Will, his face appearing at Gafferty's feet as he hurriedly pulled himself up on the rope. He scrambled on to the seat cushion as if he were being chased by some terrible monster. A huge round face emerged behind him. It smiled delightedly at the tiny people, a gigantic dollop of snot trickling down its nose.

'It's a *todla*!' gasped Gafferty. She hadn't seen it crawling along the floor behind Noah. 'All three of the Great Perils in one house!'

'She looks harmless enough to me,' said Crumpeck.

'Harmless? My little brother Grub isn't harmless, and he's a hundred times smaller than that … thing!'

Rosie giggled and placed her podgy hands on the sofa to hold herself up. Then she sneezed, the blast of warm mucus knocking them off their feet.

'I didn't think today could get any worse,' said Gafferty, getting up and wiping snot off her hoodie.

Noah reappeared, carrying something carefully.

'I'll have to be quick. Auntie Carol will be here soon to look after Rosie while Mum goes to work. I'm going with her.' He sat down on the sofa and laid the object in front of them.

'It's my glider!' said Will, his face brightening for the first time in a while. He dodged one of Rosie's grasping hands and ran to inspect it.

'I rescued it from the lettuce and brought it home,' said Noah. He looked a little embarrassed. 'Unfortunately, Rosie's been playing with it. I think she broke something.'

'One of the wing supports is damaged, that's all,' said Will happily. 'I can easily fix that with a bit of time.'

'Thank you,' Gafferty said to Noah. 'If only it could support all three of us, then we'd get home easily.'

'All three?' said Noah. 'There's only two of you here now. What happened to your friend?'

They looked around. Apart from a puddle of mucus and cat hair, all trace of Crumpeck had vanished.

14

No Return

'There he is!' said Noah. 'On the window sill.'

Crumpeck was running to the open window. He must have jumped from the sofa on to the curtain. It was made from a thick velvety material, the tufted fabric easy to grip on to for someone small.

'The crafty old sly-toes!' raged Gafferty. 'He ran the moment we were distracted!'

Noah picked Will and Gafferty up and lifted them across to the sill. Crumpeck had already clambered down into the street outside.

'There's a bus stop here!' Gafferty said, recognising the tall metal sign. 'That's why Crumpeck took a diversion through this Big Folk house. He knew there was an alternative way to get to the bus that's going to the Burrow.'

'It'll be here any minute,' said Noah. 'My auntie will be on it.' Just as he spoke the bus turned into the road.

'We have to get to that stop before the bus,' said Gafferty. 'We can't let Crumpeck get on it.'

'Why?' said Noah. 'Where's he going?'

'We don't have time to explain – we've got to go *now*!'

'But you'll never reach the stop in time,' said the boy.

'You could carry us!'

'I'm not supposed to leave the house without Mum. She's busy upstairs and I need to watch Rosie.'

'We could fly in the glider if it wasn't broken,' said Will.

'I've a better idea,' said Noah.

He picked up a piece of drawing paper and began folding it as quick as his fingers would allow. Within seconds, he had made a simple paper aeroplane.

'If you hang on to this, I could throw you out of the window,' he said.

Gafferty flinched at the thought, but for once Will was keen.

'Yes!' he said. 'I reckon I could control the flight path by pulling on the wings. This could work, Gafferty!'

Gafferty would have loved to argue, but there wasn't time. The bus was braking as it reached the stop. She could see Crumpeck hanging on to the side of an old lady's shopping trolley, ready to sneak on board. They had to go now.

'OK,' she said. 'Let's do this.'

Noah lowered the plane on to the sill so they could climb on to it. Will lay on his belly at the front, while Gafferty stretched out behind him, keeping their weight balanced.

'Hold on tight,' said Noah, as he gently lifted the plane into the air. 'And good luck!'

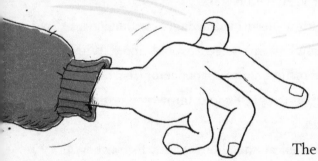

The launch was as sick-making as Gafferty had expected. The paper craft left Noah's hand and zoomed upwards, air rushing over them so fast Gafferty

had to shut her eyes, her arms almost pulled from their sockets with the force of the throw. Gafferty thought she was about to lose her grip when the plane reached the top of its rise and began to descend rapidly. Noah's aim was good, and they zipped downwards to the bus stop, Will expertly adjusting their path with tugs on the plane's wings. They came to bumpy halt just by the stop's metal signpost, the jolt buckling the plane and sending them sprawling over the concrete. Gafferty rolled several times before coming to rest face down in the dirt, her head still spinning as she got to her feet. Will was nearby, bruised but otherwise unharmed.

'That's three flights I've taken with you,' she said as she helped him up, 'and three crashes. Let's stick to land travel from now on.'

'Does that include travelling by bus?' said Will. 'Because it looks like that might be our only chance to catch Crumpeck!'

The bus had come to a standstill and the passengers had got off. The old lady was now attempting to get aboard, her short legs struggling to bridge the gap between the kerb and the vehicle.

'Hurry!' cried Gafferty. 'He mustn't get on it!'

They raced to the woman's shopping trolley, not caring if they were seen. Crumpeck still clung to its side. He didn't seem surprised to see them but also didn't seem to be about to give up.

'Crumpeck!' called Gafferty. 'Get down from there! You're already in so much trouble! If you do this, you'll be in even more. I'll personally feed you to Bogbrush, the fishmonger's cat!'

'Come back home,' said Will, more gently. 'Then we can talk about this. I'm sure Lady Strigida will understand.'

'No, she won't!' snapped Crumpeck. He gripped the

trolley more tightly. The woman had hauled herself on to the bus and was now trying to drag her shopping on behind her, unaware of the drama taking place at her feet. 'No one listens to me. I'm never appreciated. But now I've got my chance. Adventure! Discovery! Glory! Once I've found the pieces of the Mirror, they'll start paying attention. Oh yes they will!'

'This is stupid!' yelled Gafferty. 'I'm coming up there, Crumpeck. You'll be nothing but feathers when I'm finished with you!'

Before Will could stop her, she made a running jump on to the rubber wheel of the trolley, just as the woman heaved it off the ground. The wheel spun, sending Gafferty flying into Crumpeck as the trolley was wheeled into the interior of the bus. Gafferty gasped in alarm as she heard the hiss of the doors closing behind them. Too soon! This wasn't meant to happen! She pushed Crumpeck away and jumped down to the floor. Through the door's strip of glass, she saw Will's horrified face staring at them, his hands raised in frustration and despair. He shouted something, but she couldn't hear him over the noise of the bus.

'Will!' she cried. She pummelled her fist uselessly against the glass but she could only watch him disappear into the distance as the bus drove off.

She turned to see Crumpeck cowering under a seat, hiding behind a discarded drink can. Fortunately, there were few passengers, so they could easily avoid being discovered. Gafferty slumped on to the floor beside him. She was suddenly exhausted. There was no more fight left in her, no more energy left for arguing.

'Now what?' was all she said.

'Next stop, the golf course,' Crumpeck said meekly. 'Next stop, the Burrow.'

15

An Odd Meeting

'I don't like this,' said the ghost. 'It's creepy.'

'How can someone dead think something else is creepy?' said Claudia.

'It just is,' said Hinchsniff obstinately.

'He's right,' muttered Totherbligh, his bottle fidgeting at Claudia's neck. 'It's broad daylight. You don't have clandestine meetings with mysterious clients in daylight. It's not natural. There should be badly lit rooms with creaky floorboards, cobwebs and shadows.'

The post office sorting room was not, Claudia had to admit, a particularly likely setting, but it was what the client had requested. She'd had mixed feelings about returning to the funny little town that was the scene of her defeat by the Smidgens, and had reluctantly checked back into the hotel where she had almost – but not quite – obtained a piece of the Mirror. There were lots of bad memories here. But she had work to do.

The postal workers were on their lunch break, so with the help of a lock picker it had been easy to slip inside without being seen. The client had sent a note saying there was a forgotten storeroom at the back of the office, and they were to meet there.

Claudia quickly found the storeroom behind the parcels and sacks of letters. She carefully opened the door and peered inside.

'That's more like it,' said Hinchsniff.

The room was bigger than she expected and had been used more as a dumping ground than a storeroom. It was a graveyard of old machinery, boxes of franking stamps, and even some ancient postal worker uniforms. Crates were piled high on metal shelves, so that the room resembled a forest of thick, square tree trunks. It was indeed shadowy and still, and satisfyingly cobwebby. There was a sinister, watchful atmosphere that sent a chill through her.

'Hello?' she said.

'You're late.' The voice was a man's: old – very

old – raspy, and with a strange echo, as if the person were speaking from a distance. Claudia's sharp eyes darted from shadow to shadow to find its source. There was a figure, half hidden behind one of the shelves. Claudia could make out a heavily built shape, but the face was shrouded in darkness.

'I'm here now,' she said evenly, stepping forward.

'Stay where you are. I wish my identity to remain secret.'

Claudia reluctantly retreated.

'I was expecting to learn of some progress in your task,' the voice said, 'but you have been silent. I felt we should meet so you had a chance to explain.'

'I was extremely close to obtaining one of the pieces of the Mirror,' Claudia began. 'I've discovered it is held by a Smidgen called Gafferty Sprout—'

'Sprout?' said the shadow. He sounded surprised. 'You're sure it was Sprout?'

'Yes. She's tough and brave. The Smidgens are not to be underestimated.'

'I'm well aware of that. Does she still have the fragment?'

'As far as I know. Do you have any other information that could be of use? I don't have much to go on.'

Claudia's fingers ran over the bottles. Could it finally be time for her to release one of the seekers after their long period of imprisonment? Get him to spy on the client without their knowing? It would be unprofessional, and she'd always prided herself on her professionalism. This assignment had cost her so much already. She lowered her hand. The client was talking.

'I once knew so much ... but I am not the person I used to be. My body is weak. My mind is not always at its best. Sometimes I think I have seen things ... and they turn out to be merely dreams. Or, at least, I think they are ...'

He was rambling. Was he talking to her or to himself? It was difficult to tell. She had to know more. Claudia's hand reached for Hinchsniff's bottle and quietly released the ghost into the room.

'You said there were three fragments of the Mirror to find,' she prompted. 'Have you any idea of where the other two might be?'

'I remember ... three pieces, three clans. They must have divided the pieces between the clan houses, but where are they? Everything is in such a tangle.'

'Try and remember. These houses – are they obvious? We followed the Sprout girl underground for a while.

Could they be underground?'

'Underground!' The voice brightened, regained some of its strength. 'A burrow. Yes – one of the houses was underground, I'm sure of it. Outside the town, there's a place of open ground where Big Folk go to play their stupid sport ...'

'I passed a golf course on the way here,' said Claudia. Did he say *Big Folk*?

'Yes – that's it. One of the clans lived there, underground, or at least, they did at one time. You must look there.'

There was a flash of blue sparks from the shadowy figure, and an unearthly screech. Hinchsniff careered back towards Claudia, his ghostly form smoking and boiling. His weaselly face was filled with terror.

'I tried to creep up on him,' he wheezed, 'but I couldn't get close. It was like there was an invisible wall. When I touched it, it sent a horrible shock right through me!'

He slunk straight back into the bottle, pulling the stopper shut behind him.

'That's just what that Smidgen's knife did to me in the toy shop!' said Totherbligh with a shudder.

'I said not to come any closer!' It was the client, his voice shaking with anger. 'I know all about your phantom helpers, Slymark. Do not think you can use them against me! Now, leave – and do not contact me again unless you have results.'

Claudia didn't wait to argue. She ran out into the office, past the surprised postal workers coming back from their break, and out into the alley through which she had arrived. The client was a magic user of some sort. This complicated things.

'What did you see?' she asked Hinchsniff. 'What did he look like?'

'That's just it!' snivelled the ghost, still smarting. 'There was just a sack of letters with an old uniform draped over it. It might have looked like a person from where you are standing, but in reality, there wasn't anyone there at all ...'

16

The Last Straw

Gafferty awoke to find herself curled up on the floor of the bus, her head resting on a forgotten sweet still wrapped in its foil. She couldn't have been asleep long, as the bus was still moving. Crumpeck was sat beside her, his head in his hands. He looked miserable, but then he deserved to be. *Let him sulk*, thought Gafferty.

She felt like sulking too. How she wished she had made it up with Will before being trapped on this stupid bus! At least he'd been speaking to her. The argument with Wyn had been so silly, and Will had been caught in the middle of it. Wyn had been right (though he hadn't needed to be so mean about it): she did cause trouble, the same kind of trouble that

Crumpeck caused. She was annoyed with him for the same reasons others were annoyed with her. What a mess it all was!

She was hungry, and realised that Will still had the bag of food that Mum had given them to make up for missing middle-meal. That made her sulkier still. She peeled the metal foil away from the sweet, but it was a toffee, rock hard and impossible for a Smidgen to eat. There didn't appear to be anything else edible close to hand.

'I don't suppose you remembered to bring any food with you on this great expedition of yours?' she said.

Crumpeck shook his head.

'This hasn't gone how I planned it,' he said. 'Not in any way. I thought everyone would understand. I thought you would understand.'

'Me?'

'You're a risk-taker, an adventurer. Taking chances for something better. I thought you'd jump at the opportunity to dive into the unknown, to search for the third clan, regardless of what anyone else thinks.'

'When it was just us Sprouts, you had to think on your feet more,' she said. 'That was part of surviving. But it's not just us now – there's the Roost too. People who can help us, and we can help them. We don't need to take so many chances, especially if they put people in danger. Watching you make all the mistakes I've made and the trouble that puts people to – it's made me see I can't do that any more. As much as I might fight against it, we need to work together. Luck won't always be in your favour. And then you need your friends.' Friends like Will, even Noah.

'I suppose you're right. Perhaps I have been hasty.' Crumpeck's face brightened. 'But we're on our way now, so we may as well have a look for the Burrow.'

'No, we will not!' Honestly, Crumpeck was exasperating! 'You haven't been listening to a word I said! The bus will turn around and go back into town. We'll stay on it and go back with it. Is that clear?'

Crumpeck nodded obediently. Gafferty didn't trust him at all.

The bus finally drew to a stop. The door opened, and the old lady with the shopping trolley got out. There were no other passengers. The driver switched off the engine and put his feet up on the steering wheel. He had time for a nap before the return journey.

From under the seat, they could see through the open door to the entrance of the golf course. There was a huge sign over the gateway with a picture of one of the Big Folk waving a thin stick over his shoulder. That must be the golf club Gobkin had talked about. Gafferty thought something a bit bigger would be needed to hit a ball about, but humans liked to make things difficult for themselves.

Crumpeck stayed seated but gazed at the gateway wistfully.

'Where's my knife?' Gafferty said suddenly. She'd been so caught up in the chase she'd forgotten why she was chasing him. 'You can give it back to me now.'

Crumpeck's eyes lit up. *There it is*, thought Gafferty. *There's that look which means I know I can't trust him. He's hungry … hungry for the Mirror and its power, and it's making him do stupid things.*

As if he could hear her, Crumpeck sprang to his feet without a word and sprinted to the open door. He jumped straight out, despite the huge drop, and crash-landed on to the kerb outside. He staggered upright, quickly checked himself over and made off for the gateway.

'Crumpeck, stop!' Gafferty hissed, but she knew it was useless. She ran to the door and carefully lowered herself out on to the pavement, then scampered after the Smidgenologist. This was the last straw! She'd given him enough chances. Now she was going to catch him and take the knife from him, even if it meant ripping the feathered coat from his back!

A path led from the gateway to a low, square building which had the words *Club House* written over the door. The door was ajar and Crumpeck slipped through.

Gafferty followed him down the path, keeping a wary eye out. Before she reached the doorway, she glanced to one side and caught sight of what she guessed was the course itself. A vast ocean of grass, it went on as far as she could see. She'd never imagined anything like it – so much green! And every blade the same height, chopped to a blunt edge. The sameness, the lack of any flowers or weeds, was unnerving. Could there really be Smidgens living here? She hurried onwards, stealing through the door just as Crumpeck had.

The room inside resembled the foyer of the hotel, with a big desk at one side. A woman sat at the desk, flicking through some papers. Perhaps the Big Folk paid for games of golf, like they paid for rooms at the hotel? Gafferty ran for the cover of a large potted palm tree that stood beside the desk. Peering out from her hiding place, she watched Crumpeck skirting the edge of the room. She knew what he was doing: he was searching for Smidgen doors, for a secret entrance to the Burrow.

He paused for a moment underneath a glass-doored cabinet that was filled with enormous silver cups. The wall behind the cabinet was decorated in wooden panels, thin strips that ran up from the floor. Gafferty saw him examining one of the strips – it was slightly skewed, leaving a narrow gap. There was a hole in the wall.

She darted out from the cover of the palm tree and raced towards the cabinet. Crumpeck was trying to shove the panel further to one side to get a better look at the hole. He saw her approaching.

'Leave me alone!' he hissed, but she ignored him. Just as she reached his side, the panel lurched sideways. There was a snapping sound, and something landed on them, falling from the cabinet above. It was a net, like the type used to hold oranges, but weighted by pebbles. A trap! It pinned them to the floor as they struggled to free themselves, but the plastic mesh was unbreakable and the more they pulled at it, the more entangled they became.

Something stuck its head from out of the hole. It was a mouse! It studied them closely with its beady eyes as they lay there helplessly. Then it did something they weren't expecting. It spoke.

'You're my prisoners,' said the mouse.

17

Quigg

The two Smidgens stared back at the creature. Gafferty had never been this close to a mouse before, talking or otherwise. She wasn't sure whether she should be afraid or not.

'What did you say?' she eventually asked.

'You're my prisoners,' the mouse repeated. 'Are you stupid or something?'

It stepped out of the hole and stood over them on its hind legs. It gave Crumpeck a prod with a stick it was carrying.

'Get away, you horrible thing!' he shrieked.

'Calm down,' said the mouse irritably. Then, to their horror, it began to pull at its own head, as if trying to remove it. Gafferty realised it was a kind of hat, complete with large ears, and underneath the hat was …

'A girl!' she gasped. 'You're a Smidgen girl!'

'Now I definitely know you're stupid,' said the girl. 'Of course I'm a Smidgen. Just like you. Little people, big heart.'

Little people, big heart. Gafferty liked that. It sounded a bit like Dad's saying: *Too small to cause any trouble, but big enough to care.*

'You're Outsiders,' said the girl, 'caught in my door trap. That makes you *my* prisoners. I have to take you to the Chief, who'll decide what to do with you.'

She gave Crumpeck another prod to show she meant business. He squeaked, sounding more like a mouse than she did. Gafferty watched her as she skilfully untangled the net from their hands and feet. She must have been about Gafferty's age and was wearing what looked like a fur coat, but the coat was in fact made from plastic grass, the kind of fake grass that Big Folk smothered the ground with when they couldn't be bothered to grow real grass. Gafferty thought it looked much better as a coat, which this Smidgen had cleverly dyed mouse brown.

'What's your name?' she asked the girl.

'I'm asking the questions,' the girl growled.

'Sorry,' said Gafferty, standing up. 'I wanted to know who our captor was. You'll be famous once everyone hears you've caught some Outsiders in your trap.'

The girl gave this some thought and then said: 'I'm Quigg.'

'And you're from the Burrow?'

'Of course, I am. Where else could I be from? You really do say a lot of daft things.'

Crumpeck perked up at the mention of the Burrow.

'I did it!' he said. 'I found the Burrow! You see, Gafferty – it was worth it in the end.'

'Was it?' said Gafferty angrily. 'We seem to be prisoners, in case you hadn't noticed. I'm not sure that was a good result after travelling all this way. We might never get back home to tell anyone about your amazing discovery. What then?'

Crumpeck whimpered.

'I hadn't really given much thought to what would happen next,' he said.

Quigg was watching them, puzzled.

'Wait,' she said. 'You mean you really are Outsiders? I thought this was just pretend. A practice drill. I'm in training to be a tunnel guard.'

'We're from the other Smidgen clans,' said Gafferty. 'I'm Gafferty Sprout from the Hive Clan, and this is Crumpeck from the Roost Clan. We have been looking for the Burrow, but … well, this isn't how it should have happened.' She glared at Crumpeck.

Quigg tightened her grip on the stick and waved it at them threateningly.

'In that case, you really are

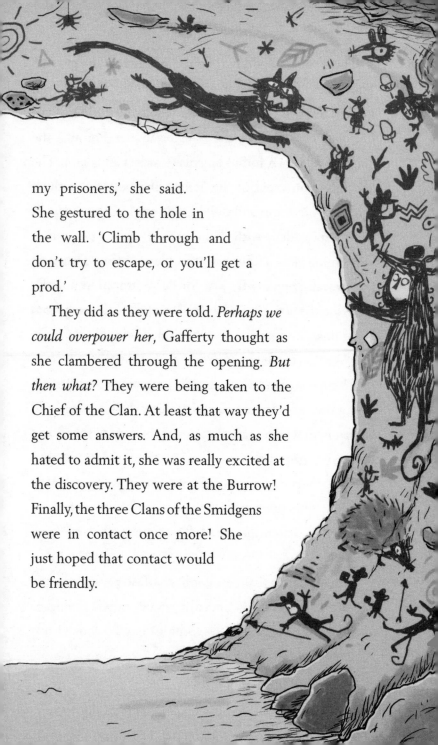

my prisoners,' she said.
She gestured to the hole in
the wall. 'Climb through and
don't try to escape, or you'll get a
prod.'

They did as they were told. *Perhaps we
could overpower her*, Gafferty thought as
she clambered through the opening. *But
then what?* They were being taken to the
Chief of the Clan. At least that way they'd
get some answers. And, as much as she
hated to admit it, she was really excited at
the discovery. They were at the Burrow!
Finally, the three Clans of the Smidgens
were in contact once more! She
just hoped that contact would
be friendly.

There were steps down from the hole into the ground. They found themselves in a winding tunnel. Gafferty was used to tunnels – she'd spent her whole life in them – but this was nothing like the Tangle. To the Sprouts, the Tangle was a dark, forbidding place, airless and damp. The less time you spent in the Tangle, the better. But these tunnels were warm and well lit. The sandy-coloured walls were embedded with light stones that gave out a welcoming glow. Other brightly coloured stones were set in the walls, apparently just for decoration. The tunnels were looked after, dry, with fresh air piped through from some unseen source. *Perhaps the Tangle was like this once, long ago*, she thought. *Perhaps it could be again.*

There were wall paintings too. Pictures of Smidgens in the guise of various animals: mice, like Quigg, and squirrels, moles and rats. Pictures of them with spears and clubs and other weapons. Some of the Smidgens looked like they were riding actual rats! Gafferty began to be worried. The Burrow Clan looked fierce. Maybe there was a good reason the other clans lived so far away from them.

Quigg marched them along at a fast pace. Soon the passageway widened, and they saw other Smidgens coming from other tunnels, Smidgens who looked just like those in the wall paintings. Their furry animal clothing was made from wool and other scraps of fabric, plastic bags or grass, like Quigg's. They stared at the strangers in their home.

'I've got prisoners!' Quigg said loudly, as she hurried her captives onwards. '*My* prisoners. They're Outsiders, real Outsiders – and I caught them!'

There were mutters of astonishment from the Burrow Clan as they passed. People looked suspicious or afraid, and young Smidgens ran to their parents for safety. It was not at all like when Gafferty had met the Roost Clan. They had been curious, but sympathetic and kind. This clan was hostile.

Gafferty felt like they'd walked for ages, and Crumpeck looked like he was about to collapse from exhaustion when they arrived at an enormous cave, a hall whose high ceiling arced overhead in a smooth dome. From it hung several golf balls studded with light-stones that acted as glitterball chandeliers. A firepit sat in the middle of the hall, behind which stood a chair, made from a leather golfing glove. A chair that was obviously meant for a very important person, with its tall back decorated with the circle, the symbol of the Burrow. Quigg prodded them towards a small room to one side.

'In here,' she said roughly. 'This is where you'll be kept until the Chief is ready to see you.'

'And then what?' said Gafferty. 'Will he let us go back home?'

Quigg shook her head.

'No,' she said flatly. 'One thing is certain. You will never see your home again.'

18

Where There's a Will, There's a Way

Claudia's car sped along the country lanes in the direction of the golf course. She tried to keep her attention on the road despite all the many questions racing through her mind.

Who or what was her mysterious client? Not a collector, that was for sure. He wanted the Mirror for a purpose. Was he some kind of magic user, one who was skilled at disappearing acts? How did he know about her seekers? And was he ill? He was behaving erratically, and seemed distracted and vague. Claudia sighed. Her life should not be as complicated as this.

She parked in the car park and warily approached the golf club entrance. There weren't many people about, thankfully. It wasn't good to have too many witnesses when you were up to mischief. She slipped through the door while the receptionist's back was turned and tiptoed through the building. Down one corridor there was a restaurant and bar, which had a scattering of diners, too many for her to search for Smidgens without looking suspicious. She retreated and tried another corridor. It had offices and storage rooms, quiet, out-of-the-way places. Claudia unstopped her seekers.

'We're looking for Smidgen activity,' she said. 'Mouseholes, crevices and crannies – anything tunnel-like.'

The ghosts flew off in different directions, sliding behind cupboards and underneath rugs, their cold fingers exploring spaces out of sight. Claudia waited impatiently, loitering by a storeroom.

A boy appeared at the end of the passage, a satchel hanging from his shoulder. He marched straight up to her and stood in front of her with his arms folded.

'What are you doing here?' he said. 'I don't think you're allowed to be here unless you work at the golf club.' Children unnerved Claudia. They were unpredictable. And this one was bossy too.

'You're a bit young to be working here yourself,' she said irritably.

'Well, I do work here, so there. My name's Noah. My mum is a cleaner at the club, and I pick up all the lost golf balls from the green while she's on her shift. The manager pays me for each one. There are loads of them. You wouldn't believe how terrible some people are at golf.'

Claudia tried to smile in a way she thought was friendly.

'Then you must be quite rich,' she said.

'I have to give all the money to my mum,' confided Noah. 'She's very high maintenance.'

'You must also know the golf course really well,' said Claudia. 'Have you ever seen anything ... unusual? Anything strange?'

'What do you mean?' said Noah. 'There are a lot of strange people here, if you ask me. Some of the players look like they've got dressed in the dark inside a clown's wardrobe.'

'Strange as in ... magical. Little people coming out of holes in the wall or holes in the ground, that kind of thing.'

The boy looked at Claudia like she had just eaten a golf ball.

'Can't say that I have,' he said, taking a step backwards. 'But if it's holes you're looking for, you're in the right place.'

'What do you mean?'

'This is a golf course. There are eighteen holes out there on the green. You can't miss them, they've all got flags in them.'

Claudia strode out of the building and on to the course.

'Keep an eye on that boy,' she said to Hinchsniff. 'He's up to something.'

Noah watched the woman leave, followed by an odd trail of mist.

'She's gone!' he said to no one. 'Was that her? Claudia Slymark?'

Willoughby's worried face peeped out from the satchel where he'd been hiding.

'Yes!' he said. 'And she's still looking for Smidgens. I don't need this, along with all our other problems.'

'It was lucky you spotted her,' said Noah. 'And the ghosts! I'd never have believed they existed. This is turning into a very weird day. Anyway, the course is huge. It should keep her busy while we search for Gafferty.'

'If only you'd said your mum worked here.' Will

sighed. 'It would have saved us a lot of trouble with that bus. We could have come with you in the *kar*.'

'I might have told you, but you were too busy arguing with each other to listen.'

'We've been arguing all day. It's been horrible. What if I don't see Gafferty again? I'll never get to say sorry.'

He climbed out of the bag and on to Noah's waiting hand.

'Then we'd better start looking,' said the boy. 'The cupboards first? Or the maintenance room?'

'We could try the restaurant,' said Will thoughtfully. 'Smidgens have to eat, so they must have a Smidgen door there somewhere. Gafferty would know where to look.'

'Wait – what about the Crazy Golf course? It's made to look like a little town – all the holes are buildings, just the right size for a Smidgen to live in. I bet you'll find this other clan in there.'

Noah let Will sit on his shoulder and took him through a side and door out of the club house. Will's jaw dropped at the sight before him. The Crazy Golf play area did look just like a Smidgen-sized version of a Big Folk town, with little houses, a lake and even, Will saw with a jolt of envy, a pizza restaurant. He knew no Smidgen would ever live somewhere so exposed to human eyes, especially when there were golf balls regularly hurtling through the holes in each of the buildings, but it was possible they were doorways to the Burrow.

Noah put Will down next to the nearest building, a flower shop with painted windows. The Smidgen peered through the hole in its wall. It was very dark, and very cold. Will felt like someone was watching him. His tummy churned nervously. He had to be brave.

'Think like Gafferty,' he said aloud as he stepped inside.

'I wouldn't if I were you,' hissed a ghostly voice. 'It will only lead to trouble …'

19

the Great Jewel

Gafferty and Crumpeck hadn't been locked in the room for long when Quigg reappeared, carrying a tray with water and some breadcrumbs.

'You're not so unfriendly after all,' said Gafferty, taking a breadcrumb eagerly.

'Why would we be?' said Quigg, putting the tray on the floor, and pulling her stick from her belt. 'Little people, big heart. You're the Outsiders. You're the troublemakers. You're in here to keep everyone else safe.'

'We're Smidgens too! Our hearts are just as big as yours. And we're not troublemakers. We only came her because we wanted to be friends.' *And not because one of us is after a magical mirror*, Gafferty thought. She gave

Crumpeck an extra glare just in case he was thinking of saying something. The Smidgenologist sat forlornly on the floor, silently chewing on a breadcrumb. He'd not spoken since they'd been caught.

Quigg studied them carefully. She had a stern face for someone young, thoughtful and wary.

'You're certainly a bit too pathetic-looking to be troublemakers,' she said after a moment. 'The way you got caught in that net was ridiculous. But that could have been a trick to make me think you're harmless. All the stories say we should keep away from the other clans, that they can't be trusted.'

'What stories?' said Gafferty. She thought of the pictures painted on the Burrow walls. Could they tell part of the history of the Smidgens?

'The stories of the old times. Before the Great Jewel came to us. It was born out of the war between the clans, and now we protect it from you lot. Don't you know?'

'No. I've never heard of any of this!' Gafferty frowned. The Burrow Smidgens seemed to know a lot more about the past than anyone at the Roost or her own family. Unless the truth had been deliberately hidden from them. She remembered Mum saying that people write the history they want to remember and leave out the parts they don't like. Gafferty had thought it was impossible for a Smidgen to be bad, and now she had found out that in the past Smidgens had even fought other Smidgens. A war between the clans? Could it be true?

'Did you say *the Great Jewel*?' Crumpeck said quietly. He had perked up after his breadcrumb.

'Yes. Don't pretend you don't know about it. I bet it warned the Chief you were coming, which is why he ordered that security drill.'

'The jewel warned him?' said Gafferty. 'You mean it talks?'

'That's enough questions!' snapped Quigg. 'The Chief wants to see you now, and he'll have plenty of questions for *you*.'

She brandished her stick at them, and they hurried out into the great hall. The room had filled with Smidgens while they'd been locked up. Some were sitting on golf tees that had been pushed into the earth next to the throne. On the throne itself sat a rotund Smidgen with a long beard, dressed in a black velvet coat with large gloves on his hands, so that he looked like a plump mole.

Quigg herded Gafferty and Crumpeck until they were standing in front of him.

'Chief Talpa,' said Quigg proudly, 'these are my prisoners, who I caught all by myself. They are self-confessed Outsiders who infiltrated the perimeter at the Great Big Folk Door. They claim they only want to be *friends*.' She said the word with a sneer, and the other Smidgens laughed.

'Why would you laugh when someone offers you friendship?' said Gafferty.

'Silence, Outsider!' roared Chief Talpa.

'No, I won't be silent!' said Gafferty. She was angry and fed up. 'It's been a really long, stupid day, and this has got to be the stupidest part of it. If two Smidgens turned up at my door saying they wanted to be friends, I'd invite them in, offer them some cake crumbs and maybe even a bit of chocolate, if my little brother hadn't eaten it all. We'd sit down and have a chat. So far, I've been caught in a net, prodded with a stick and locked in a room for absolutely no reason. That's a bit rubbish, all in all.'

'Silence!' raged the Chief.

'NO!' shouted Gafferty. 'You should be ashamed of yourselves. *Little people, big heart* – that's your saying, and that's what I think Smidgens are too. But all I've seen here are small *minds* and *no* heart.' She folded her arms, and glared at the Chief, who was so red with anger he

132

looked like a tomato wearing an overcoat.

'How dare you?' he spat furiously. 'Insolent child! You've no right to speak to me like that. The Smidgens from outside the Burrow caused all the problems to start with. You've got a nerve coming here and asking to be friends when your lot broke the bonds of friendship in the first place.'

'I don't know what you're talking about but I'm sure you must be wrong …'

'Wrong?' Chief Talpa got to his feet and grabbed Gafferty by the arm. 'Follow me and we'll see who's wrong, girl.'

'Let go!' yelled Gafferty, but he was too strong for her. The Chief dragged her from the hall, trailed by Crumpeck, Quigg and a huddle of shocked Smidgens. He released her as they reached a small circular room that glowed with a light Gafferty recognised. Soft and rose-coloured, it was exactly the same light that radiated from her knife. There in front of them, standing on a pedestal in the middle of the room and surrounded by intricate wall paintings, was a large piece of crystal, about the size of a Smidgen child. A section of its edge was a smooth curve, as if it had been part of larger circular or oval object. The other edges were ragged and cracked.

'Behold the Great Jewel!' said Chief Talpa. 'The most sacred object in the Smidgenverse!'

Both Gafferty and Crumpeck stared. They knew exactly what it was: not a jewel, but another piece of the Mirror of Trokanis! A huge piece that the Burrow had on display to everyone. *It's been safely hidden under the golf course for all these years*, thought Gafferty. *What would Claudia Slymark do if she knew this was here? It's a good job she left the town and didn't come back.*

Before she could say anything, Crumpeck had reached inside his coat and produced the knife. Gafferty's heart leaped when she saw it, as if a missing part of her had suddenly been rediscovered. He raised the knife in the air, and it began to glow, spots of light emerging from its core, just like they had done when Gafferty had held it aloft in the Smidgenmoot when she first met Will. More spots appeared, this time from the Great Jewel, and they spun around each other, faster and faster. The two pieces of glass began to tremble, and a humming sound filled the chamber, a sound that suddenly erupted into a chorus of voices, shouting and talking at once, creating a surging wave of sound. The last thing Gafferty remembered was the shock wave knocking them off their feet and sending them flying across the room.

20

Ghostly Golf

'If it isn't Gafferty Sprout's pathetic little flying friend,' sneered Hinchsniff. Will stood quaking inside the little wooden flower shop as the ghost slowly circled him. 'The last time I saw you, you were about to plummet to your death from a tall building. It looks like you survived. What a shame ...'

'I survived, thanks to Gafferty,' Will stammered. 'It's not so bad being like her sometimes.'

'Ha! We'll see about that. But if you're here, that means she must be nearby. And other Smidgens too – which is just what my mistress is hoping for. I'd better take you with me – I'm sure she'd like to have a little chat with you herself.'

Will didn't wait to hear any more. He dived out of the flower shop and ran as fast as he could through the pretend town. Sometimes running away was better than being brave – he was sure that Gafferty's Rules had *run for it* in them somewhere. He glanced around the empty course. Where was Noah?

Hinchsniff slowly uncurled itself from inside the little building.

'You won't get far, boy,' he called. 'I'm not in any hurry. I've been stuck inside my bottle for so long I plan to enjoy the time I'm free. And when I find you I'm going to enjoy freezing you very, very slowly. I'm going to enjoy it very much indeed.'

His vaporous form glided in and out of the buildings. Will watched from his hiding place inside a model lighthouse as the ghost swept past. What now? What would Gafferty do? *I wish she were here now*, he thought.

Maybe if he went back to the club house, back to where there were more people, he would be safe. He peered out of the lighthouse. He would have to cross the lake and go through the windmill. If he ran fast, he might be able to make it. Taking a deep breath, he dashed from the lighthouse door and ran to the lake. There was an arched bridge over it that the players had to drive their ball across without it falling in the water. It was quite a steep climb and Will stopped for a moment, panting, in the middle.

'Look out behind you ...'

Will turned to see a golf ball rolling towards him, pushed by a phantom hand. It was getting faster and faster, barrelling up the bridge. There was no escape – he couldn't jump aside without landing in the lake! He would have to outrace it. He charged down the other side of the bridge as the ball tumbled after him, its hard, pocked surface threatening to knock him flying. Hinchsniff chuckled gleefully at the sight.

'I always thought golf was a boring game,' he said. 'I was

obviously playing with the wrong people.'

Will had almost made it to the windmill when the ball caught him squarely in the back, knocking him to the ground, wheezing. Hinchsniff loomed over him as he crawled towards the building. If he could get to the other side, he'd almost be at the club house …

'Get away from my friend!'

A small white object burst through Hinchsniff's middle, leaving a hole going from one side of the ghost to the other. A golf ball bounced off the windmill and clattered to the ground. Will jumped up and ducked behind the building for cover.

'Who did that?' snapped the ghost, looking around. 'You can't go knocking holes through a person! It's very disrespectful!'

'I did!' Noah appeared, carrying a bucket filled to the top with golf balls. He had a club in the other hand, its head resting on his shoulder.

'Those golf balls can't hurt me, you foolish child!' sneered Hinchsniff, as the hole in his phantom tummy resealed itself. 'You'll have to do better than that!'

'Just watch!' cried Noah. 'I was the under-elevens Crazy Golf champion last year. I beat Ewan Fothergill by four strokes.'

He emptied the bucket of golf balls on the ground, swung the club behind him and then struck one ball as hard as he could. POW! It flew straight at the windmill and sailed through its door. The sails spun briskly. But Noah didn't stop there. He hit one golf ball after another, each flying through the air with surprising force, and every single one went straight through the doorway of the windmill. He wasn't lying, Will thought – he was good at this!

As each golf ball went through the door, it hit a lever that sent the windmill's wooden sails spinning round and round. They churned the air, turning the windmill into a powerful fan. Hinchsniff's form began to thin, his misty body buffeted by the breeze Noah was creating.

'What are you doing?' the ghost cried.

'I'm blowing you away like a nasty rain cloud!' said Noah.

Hinchsniff gave a startled cry – his ghostly body was starting to fall apart as the breeze pulled him further away from his magical bottle – too far. He'd have to get back to Claudia and safety. He growled nastily at them, but it was no good. He retreated, disappearing across the green.

'That was amazing, Noah!' said Will, emerging from his hiding place. 'I don't know what I would have done without you. You're not bad, for a human!'

Noah laughed for a moment but then he looked serious.

'It's not over yet,' he said. 'We don't know where your friends are, and Claudia and the ghosts are still on the loose.'

'We have to find Gafferty before Claudia does,' said Will, 'but there's so much ground to cover. This place is huge.' Then he tapped his chin and gave Noah a smile. 'But I think I might have a plan ...'

21

The Thirteenth Hole

Gafferty awoke and looked straight into the face of Quigg. Strangely, considering the things Quigg had said earlier, the girl appeared concerned, instead of glaring at Gafferty scornfully.

'What ... happened? said Gafferty. She shook her head to try and clear the buzzing from her ears. She was sitting on the floor of the chamber containing the Great Jewel, her back against the painted wall. Chief Talpa sat on the other side of the room, looking bleary-eyed and unsteady, while next to her Crumpeck lay on the floor, unconscious. The Great Jewel itself gleamed but was silent.

'You know better than us,' said Quigg. 'One minute

you were standing up, and the next minute the Great Jewel had started glowing and you, the Chief and pigeon guy were bouncing off the walls like a bunch of grasshoppers in a jam jar.'

'Didn't you hear it?' she said. 'All the voices? It was a huge noise.'

Quigg exchanged looks with the curious Smidgens who were standing behind her, and then glanced at the Chief.

'We didn't hear anything,' she said. 'You say you heard voices? Only the Chief hears the Jewel speak.'

Talpa moaned, and Quigg ran to his side. Gafferty spotted her knife on the ground next to Crumpeck. He must have dropped it when he fell. Everyone was busy fussing about the Chief, so she quickly grabbed it and stuffed it into her waistcoat. The sudden movement made her head spin, so she steadied herself by focusing on one of the paintings on the wall. This was what Talpa had meant to show her. There was a picture of a group of Burrow Smidgens carrying the jewel, painted bright pink, away from a battle between birds, insects and mice. It didn't look very violent, more like a dance, but it was clear the animals were very cross with each other. A grey bird was flying away with another pink jewel, while a spider carried a third. Was this a drawing of when the Mirror was broken? Then she noticed how brightly lit the paintings were, but there were no glow-stones nearby. Light shone from a hole in the ceiling.

'Is that daylight?' Gafferty asked. 'We're underground, aren't we?'

Quigg returned to her side.

'There's a window in the ceiling above us,' she said. 'Each of the holes on the golf course has a glass floor. The Big Folk don't know about them. We use them to light the whole of the Burrow. This room is under the thirteenth hole.'

The Chief mumbled something. He seemed anxious.

'Chief Talpa wants to talk to you,' said Quigg.

Gafferty struggled to her feet. She was a bit wobbly, but the ringing in her ears had gone.

'You heard it, didn't you?' said the Chief weakly as she knelt next to him. He didn't appear to be angry any more. 'You heard the voice of the Great Jewel.'

'I've heard something similar before,' said Gafferty. 'My knife, which Crumpeck held up, spoke to me once. I couldn't understand what it said, but I felt a connection to it. I still do.'

The Chief seemed puzzled. 'I have the gift of hearing

the voice. The gift is what makes me Chief of the Clan. The voice isn't clear, sometimes its meaning is vague, and I must try and interpret the Jewel's commands. Only members of my family have been able to hear it, ever since the time of my foremother, Gresca.' He pointed a finger at the mouse carrying the Jewel in the painting.

'Does that mean … we're related?'

The Chief chuckled.

'No,' he said. 'But you must have inherited this power. Perhaps you are descended from the others present when the Jewel was born, like Gresca. Perhaps you are descended from the spider whose disguise you wear.'

Gafferty looked again at the painting. The spider was obviously meant to be someone from the Hive. Could the Chief be right? Was an ancestor of hers there when the Mirror was broken? And perhaps they then took a piece with them back to the Hive, where it was hidden for years until Dad had stumbled across it. She had another thought.

'But there's a bird in the picture too,' she said. 'Could that mean … Could it be that Crumpeck might be descended from someone who was there too? Someone from the Roost? He obviously heard the Jewel too, just like us.'

145

That might explain Crumpeck's behaviour, his insistence on finding the Burrow. Perhaps it felt like he was being driven by outside forces, an inner voice. The Smidgenologist stirred and groaned. Quigg went to help him sit up.

'You know something about the Jewel, don't you?' the Chief whispered to Gafferty. 'What is the nature of this knife of yours?'

'The story I was told is that the knife was part of an enchanted mirror. The Mirror of Trokanis. It was some kind of magical doorway the Smidgens of the old days used. It was broken – I don't know how, but it looks like you know more about this than we do.' Gafferty paused. She was going to have to own up to the truth. 'We do want friendship with the Burrow, but we also want to find all the pieces of the Mirror, and we thought it was possible you might have one. I think that's what the Great Jewel is.'

'You want to steal the Jewel!' The Chief frowned. 'Our sacred object! We were right not to trust you!'

'No!' said Gafferty. 'You can trust us! We only want to find them before others do! Big Folk have been looking for them, a woman named Claudia Slymark. I don't know why she wants the Mirror, but she's very dangerous and doesn't care what happens to Smidgens.'

There was a commotion from outside in the great hall. Gafferty could hear shouting, some screams. Quigg ran out to investigate, followed by the other Smidgens. There were more shouts, louder and closer.

'What's going on?' said Talpa. Gafferty helped him stagger to his feet. They left Crumpeck still dazed in the chamber and wandered as quickly as they could towards the hall. There was an agitated conversation taking place between Quigg and another scared-looking Smidgen in a mouse coat similar to hers.

'What are you talking about, Bungo?' Quigg was saying. 'Monsters? What monsters?'

'Terrible things!' said Bungo. 'Horrible creatures – they've got into the Burrow! The window of the twelfth hole was smashed from above and the creatures poured in. When anyone tries to stop them, they just surround them and freeze them. They look like they're made of mist, or like they might even be—'

'Ghosts,' said Gafferty, her voice quiet with dread. 'They're ghosts.'

22

Claudia Strikes Back

'It's Claudia Slymark, the woman I told you about,' Gafferty said, turning to the Chief. 'Somehow she's found out about the Burrow. The ghosts work for her.'

'You led her here!' said Talpa. 'You've betrayed us!'

'I didn't! I haven't!' Gafferty found she was fighting back tears. She was exhausted, not just from the journey, but from arguing with people she thought should know better – her own people. It was so frustrating and pointless.

Before she could say anything else, there were more shouts, and half a dozen Smidgens came running into the hall followed by a stream of smoke. The smoke surrounded the nearest Smidgen, who halted mid-run and fell to the ground, a statue covered in a blue-white frost.

Quigg and the Chief gasped in fear at the sight of the ghost. Its body was squeezed out of shape to fit through the tunnel but in the middle of its swirling form Gafferty immediately recognised the thing's weaselly eyes as those of Hinchsniff. Then she remembered the last time she'd met the ghosts.

'They don't like my knife,' she said. 'It can hurt them. So that means they won't want to go near the Jewel. You'll be safe there.' The two Smidgens looked doubtful.

'We can't trust you!' said Talpa. 'It could be a trap!'

'You have to believe me! There isn't time to argue!'

The ghost poured through the hall, freezing Smidgen after Smidgen as it filled the room. Quigg nodded.

'We don't have any other choice,' Quigg said to Talpa. 'Let's do what she says for now.'

The Chief and Quigg hurriedly followed Gafferty back to the chamber of the Great Jewel.

'Where's the other one?' said Quigg. Crumpeck was nowhere to be seen.

'He must have followed us out,' said Gafferty, 'with all the noise and confusion.'

'Never mind him!' snapped the Chief. 'Where's the Great Jewel?'

It was gone – its pedestal stood empty! Gafferty's

heart sank. *Oh, Crumpeck – please say you haven't …*

CRACK!

The room trembled, and bits of the earth above their heads crumbled to the floor, filling the chamber with dust.

CRACK!

'What's happening now?' wailed Talpa. Suddenly a huge metal pole crashed through the skylight, splinters of glass showering around them.

'The window has been smashed!' cried Quigg, just as another misty shape billowed into the chamber from above.

'Totherbligh!' said Gafferty. The ghost saw her and grinned mischievously.

'Well, well!' he said, curling his body around the bare pedestal as the Smidgens cowered in front of him. 'What do we have here? A veritable infestation of rat folk, including the most pestilential pest of them all, little Miss Gafferty Sprout. So nice to see you again, my dear.'

Gafferty jumped in front of the others and pulled her knife from her jacket. She waved it in Totherbligh's leering face. Sparks spat from the blade and stung him like tiny biting insects. He yelped and drew back.

'Keep that thing away from me!'

'Go back to your mistress and tell her I'm going to stop her,' yelled Gafferty.

'I will,' said Totherbligh, retreating through the skylight like smoke up a chimney. 'But now she knows you're here, along with your accursed little splinter, I don't think you'll have much luck.'

Gafferty and Quigg scampered back to the hall once more, the Chief trailing behind. There were frozen Smidgens lying everywhere, but no sign of Hinchsniff.

'What's happened to them?' cried Quigg. 'Will they be all right?'

'Don't worry,' said Gafferty. 'It's called fright-freeze. It will wear off after a while. In the meantime, we must find Crumpeck! If Claudia gets to him before we do, we'll never get your Jewel back.'

There was a startled squeal from behind them. They turned and saw the Chief lying frozen on the ground, his eyes wide with surprise. A horrible chuckling floated down from over their heads.

'Hello again!' Hinchsniff sniggered. 'I thought I'd find you once we met your little bird friend.' *Bird friend?* Will! Gafferty's heart leaped. Was he here? Was he safe? There was no time to think about it.

'Run!' said Gafferty, pushing the horrified Quigg

down a passageway. She waved her knife at Hinchsniff, and he hissed at her like a snake, but thankfully didn't follow. 'Crumpeck must be trying to find his way out of here,' she said. 'Which path takes us back to the club house?'

'This way,' said Quigg, diving into a side passage. 'He can't have got far if he's carrying the Jewel. It must weigh as much as I do!'

They followed the passage. It was deserted, the Smidgens of the Burrow hiding in their homes from the strange invaders. Then they saw him, hobbling along the corridor ahead, a large object tucked under his coat. Gafferty had been hoping she was mistaken, hoping he hadn't stolen the Jewel, but there was no mistaking either him or it. Her heart sank.

'Crumpeck!' she shouted.

Just as he turned, a metal wall descended through the ceiling in front of them with a huge crash. Gafferty saw the danger and just had time to pull Quigg out of its way before she could be sliced in half. The barrier blocked off the passage and carved through the tunnel on either side. For a moment, Gafferty thought some kind of door or gateway had been shut in their faces, but from Quigg's scream she realised that wasn't the case. Just as quickly as it had fallen, the wall rose out of the ground, showering earth all over them, as daylight streamed in from above. Gafferty looked up in dismay. The metal wall was the blade of a spade – someone was digging up the Burrow! And that someone could only be Claudia Slymark.

Ahead, she saw Crumpeck staggering onwards down the passage. The spade dug into the tunnel once more, narrowly missing him but close enough in front of him to send him flying backwards, the Jewel tumbling to the ground. The spade then tore the roof off the passage, revealing them all to the sky. Claudia stood astride the tunnel, spade in hand, with a satisfied smile. She hadn't spotted Gafferty, who dragged Quigg back the way they came until they were hidden from view. She did see Crumpeck, however, and scooped him up in her hand as he desperately clung on to the Jewel.

'Buried treasure,' she said, leaning on her spade, as the Smidgenologist tried to wriggle free.

'Let me go!' squealed Crumpeck.

'No,' said Claudia. 'You and your little bauble are coming with me. And this time, I'm not going to let this precious object out of my sight.'

23

Escape from the Burrow

'Oh, Crumpeck!' Gafferty gaped in horror as Claudia tucked him and the Jewel into her bag. 'What can we do?'

'Nothing!' said Quigg. 'Except get out of here. She's after you, and she knows you're in the Burrow. If you don't want her to get her hands on your knife, you have to leave. The passage is blocked – we'll have to dig through with our hands.'

'Wait!' Gafferty pointed upwards delightedly. 'Look! It's Will – and he's flying!'

In the sky over their heads they could make out the silhouette of the training glider that Noah had rescued. Will dangled underneath it, guiding it skilfully.

'*Another* friend of yours?' said Quigg, staring at the glider in dismay. 'I hope he's got more sense than you and that other one have.'

'Not really,' said Gafferty cheerfully. 'I hope he knows what he's doing. What *is* he doing?'

Will was circling over Claudia's head. She hadn't seen him. He took the glider into a sudden dive that buzzed past her face. She jumped back in alarm. Will dived again and again, like a wasp bothering a picnic, Claudia angrily trying to swat him away.

'You little brat!' Claudia snarled. 'Do you think you're really capable of stopping me with that thing?'

'No!' Will yelled, as he took the glider in for another dive. 'But it'll keep you busy for a while.'

'Keep me busy? What do you mean, you dratted creature?'

'I mean it'll keep you busy long enough for backup to arrive!'

Gafferty and Quigg scrambled out of the crater that Claudia had made. On the horizon they saw a gigantic machine heading towards them. It was a huge lawnmower, its blades turning furiously. Sitting on top of it was a very angry man, with a boy hanging on to the seat. The boy was grinning like he was having the time of his life.

'It's Noah!' said Gafferty. 'He's helping us!'

'You're friends with Big Folk?' muttered Quigg. 'This gets worse and worse.'

There were other Big Folk behind the lawnmower. They did not look happy about their pristine golf course being dug up like a vegetable patch. Some were even waving clubs in a way that made Gafferty think golf might be a violent game after all. Claudia took one last swipe at the glider, which Will neatly avoided, before running away down the course.

'Hinchsniff! Totherbligh!' she squawked. The ghosts appeared and obediently followed her as she fled the pursuing Big Folk.

Will's glider swooped low over the Smidgens' heads. The flat green was a perfect place for a landing, and Gafferty and Quigg ran across the wide-open space to meet him, as the glider came to an uncharacteristically smooth stop.

'Will!' Gafferty hugged the boy before he'd even had time to unclip his harness. 'I'm so sorry! I hate it that we argued. I know I said some terrible things, but I didn't mean any of them! And I know I cause trouble, but I don't mean that either.'

Will grinned broadly.

'I've had to be a bit Gafferty-ish myself, lately,' he said. 'I'm sorry too, Gafferty. I should have stood up for you more. Sometimes you do just have to dive in and live dangerously – especially if you know it's the right thing to do.'

'Little people, big heart,' said Quigg. 'If we're finished with the soppy stuff, we need to get moving. When the Chief and all other Smidgens wake up from this fright-freeze they are not going to be pleased. They're going to think you helped Claudia steal the Jewel.'

'But you'll tell them we didn't, won't you?' Gafferty pleaded. 'It was Crumpeck. Something's got into him – he's not in control of what he's doing.'

'You just saved my life, so I'll help you. And I think I believe you too. But I'm not going to be telling them anything because I'm coming with you.'

'What?'

'I'm going to get the Jewel back.' Quigg had a determined frown set on her face. 'And you're going to help me find it. You have to tell me everything you know.'

Gafferty looked at her in surprise. This tough little Smidgen was not going to take no for an answer. And she could be useful. At the very least they had an ally in the Burrow.

Noah arrived, breathless but eyes shining.

'Claudia's been well and truly seen off the golf course,' he said. 'She won't be allowed back in again after the damage she's done.'

'Hopefully, that means the rest of the Burrow is safe,' said Will. 'But it sounds like she got most of what she wanted anyway.'

Noah put the glider in the satchel and the Smidgens climbed in after. Quigg was wary of the human boy, and gave his fingers a prod with her trusty stick just to show him she wasn't to be trifled with.

Gafferty and Quigg had never been in a *kar* before, and Quigg had never been beyond the golf course, so on the drive back to Noah's house they both peeked out of the satchel and watched the countryside rushing by. Gafferty was reminded again of how big the Outside was. There was so much to explore, if only she got the chance!

Back home, once he'd shut the cat out of the kitchen, Noah set the Smidgens free by the refrigerator.

'Thank you so much for your help!' said Will, shaking the boy's finger. 'I don't think I'd have found Gafferty without you.'

'Will I see you again?' said Noah, smiling shyly. 'I'd like to help you if I can.'

'Claudia's dangerous,' said Gafferty. 'And you don't want to get messed up in our problems, believe me. We owe you so much already.'

'But I need you to hang on to my glider,' said Will. 'I'll be back for it one day. And if you ever need to get in touch with us, leave a picture of a bird in your window. Someone will see it.'

Noah nodded, and with a wave, they ran behind the refrigerator and into the depths of the Tangle. Gafferty had never been so glad to see the familiar dreary tunnels!

'Where are you taking me?' said Quigg, as they followed the passageway back to the chocolate factory. 'Is this the way to the human thief's home?' She looked nervous in the dimly lit and stuffy Tangle, which was so unlike the bright, airy Burrow.

'No, we're going to my home,' said Gafferty. 'We need to let everyone know what's happened. We need to get help.'

'I can't wait to see their faces when they know we've brought back someone from the third Smidgen clan,' said Will with a grin. 'You find clans like I find holes in my socks, Gafferty. You really are made for exploring.'

'Right now, I could do with a bit less exploring and a bit more home cooking,' Gafferty replied. 'I've not had a proper meal all day, and it's almost dinner time.'

They soon reached the factory, just as the workers were going home for the day.

'You live here?' Quigg said, taking in the enormous space and strange machinery as they scampered across the factory floor. Her eyes scanned every corner, as if she were taking mental notes.

'Underneath it,' Gafferty said, suddenly feeling proud of her home. She thought it was much better than a golf course.

She and Will scrambled under the door that led into the basement as Quigg took one last look back at the factory. Then, making sure the others were out of sight, Quigg reached into her coat pocket and pulled out a small piece of thread, tying it around a loose nail sticking out of a crate. A piece of thread just like the many others she had secretly left behind her as they had travelled, in a trail that only a Burrow Smidgen would recognise.

24

The Unwelcome Houseguest

The Sprout family were astonished to see Gafferty and Will turn up for dinner with the strangely dressed Quigg.

'You were supposed to come straight back home if there was any trouble!' thundered Dad after they had explained what had happened. He and Quigg eyed each other suspiciously, while Grub tried to bite the Burrow Smidgen every time she came within range of his sharp little teeth. 'And now you tell me you've been travelling on paper wings, buses and *kars*, mixing with Big Folk children and more foreign Smidgens! Gafferty Sprout, when it comes to being irresponsible, you outdo yourself every time you walk out of that door.'

'I was trapped on the bus,' Gafferty pointed out.

'Otherwise I would have come back. I don't know what else I could have done, Dad.'

'And it's just as well we went to the Burrow,' added Will. 'Or we wouldn't have found out about Claudia Slymark being back in town and hunting for Smidgens and bits of magic glass again. I'd better go home and tell Lady Strigida what's happened. I'm not looking forward to hearing what she'll have to say about Crumpeck, but I'm sure she'll come up with a plan for what to do next.'

'We're going to get the Jewel back,' said Quigg bluntly. 'That's what we're going to do next.'

Dad grumbled as Will made his escape, but he could see that all the young Smidgens were safe and sound, so he let both girls eat. They devoured the potato-and-cheese-burgers that were put before them, and the jelly-baby heads, and the little cups of sweet tea. Mum gave Quigg's long coat a thorough brush while Gobkin pestered her with questions about the Big Folk game of golf. The girl kept her answers short and simple. She was never rude, but she wasn't exactly friendly either. The Smidgens of the Burrow seemed to have a very different attitude to everything, compared to the Sprouts or the Smidgens of the Roost, Gafferty decided. Perhaps it was because they were so isolated. It had made them cautious and distrustful. Perhaps that had influenced their version of the story of the Mirror. According to Chief Talpa, it was Outsiders who had caused the Mirror to break, Outsiders were the ones to blame for all the Smidgens' troubles. She wondered if they would ever know what really happened.

It was getting late, so Dad made up a bed for Quigg in Gafferty's room, using a matchbox and a Big Folk sock. Gafferty wasn't sure she really wanted to share space with the grumpy girl, but it would have been unkind to object.

'Goodnight, Quigg,' she said, as they settled down for the night. 'I hope everyone in the Burrow is safe. It would be wonderful if all the Smidgens could all be friends one day, don't you think?'

Quigg just sniffed and said nothing.

Gafferty wasn't sure how long she'd been asleep when she was awoken by the kitchen light flickering on, and the sound of voices, troubled and grave. She stumbled out of bed to see Will and Wyn, and their Uncle Abel, talking to Mum and Dad. Dad held a sleeping Grub, his little mouth wide open, while a drowsy Gobkin clung to Mum's hand. Wyn looked at her but didn't smile.

'You need to hear this, Gaff,' said Mum, 'and bring

that Quigg girl out here. She needs to do some explaining.'

Gafferty ran to her room, but the matchbox was empty. The sock had been folded in on itself to make it look like someone was sleeping inside.

'She's gone!' she called. 'What's happening?'

Uncle Abel didn't look surprised.

'We think she may have put us all in danger,' he said.

'I knew it!' said Dad. 'She had trouble written all over her face!'

'How has she put us in danger?' said Gafferty. 'What danger?'

'A picture of a bird was seen by one of our scouts in the window of Noah's bedroom this evening,' said Will. 'Me and Wyn flew straight there. Noah said he had seen rats sniffing about in the backyard of his house.'

'Rats? So what?'

'Rats with Smidgens on their backs! Lots of them. We didn't see anything, but Noah said they seemed to be searching for something, using the rats to follow a scent. He poked his head out of the back door and they vanished.'

'You think you were followed back here?' asked Mum, horrified. 'By the Burrow Smidgens? But you came most of the way in a Big Folk *kar*. That's too fast for a rat to follow.'

'They would have known the children were heading

for the town,' said Abel. 'Once they were here, it was just a matter of picking up the scent. Quigg may have left a trail for them.'

'But why?' said Gafferty. 'Why would she do that?'

'Their precious Jewel is gone, their people and their home have been attacked,' said Wyn, grim-faced. 'And it all started when you turned up there. They're blaming you, Gafferty, and coming for revenge.'

'That's not fair!' snapped Gafferty, her face burning. Not just burning with anger, but with the fear that Wyn might be right. This had all started when she decided to go and look for more Smidgens. She'd set everyone on this path.

Will elbowed his brother in the ribs.

'That's just nonsense!' he said. 'Gafferty's not to blame for this – if anyone is, it's Crumpeck. And anyway, if there's one thing we've learned, it's that this all comes down to stuff that happened long ago, years and years ago. It's about the past, not about what's happening now.'

Gafferty looked at him gratefully. She'd never seen him standing up to his brother before, and the fact that he was doing it on her behalf made her warm with pride.

'Will is right,' said Abel, looking sternly at his older nephew. 'This is an old story, repeating itself. The last thing we need is arguing amongst ourselves.'

Wyn looked at his feet.

'Young Wibbly might be right,' said Dad, 'but that doesn't help us now. If you think those Smidgens are coming here, and that they've not got friendly intentions, then we need to do something.'

'Lady Strigida has put the Roost on full alert,' said Abel. 'Claudia Slymark may be back at the hotel, so we've got people searching for her room. It may take some time to find her. In the meantime, everyone who has wings is getting ready to fly.'

'Fly?' said Mum. 'Fly where?'

'Fly here,' said Abel. 'The Burrow Smidgens and their rats are coming here. We don't know if they mean harm or not, and we've little time to escape.' He drew out a needle that had been secured to his belt and held it up. Its point looked sharp, cold and deadly. 'It may be that we'll have to face them in battle. Smidgen against Smidgen.'

25

A Council of War

'Fight?' said Gafferty. She couldn't believe what she was hearing. Smidgens fighting other Smidgens when the real problem was a thieving human? 'Are you serious?'

Abel couldn't have looked more serious.

'I hope it won't come to it,' he said, 'but we have to be prepared to defend ourselves, at the very least.'

'They think they're going to take us by surprise,' growled Dad. 'But we've a bit of time.' He handed the sleeping Grub to Gobkin. 'Now, son – your job is to look after your brother, while your mother guards the House. This place is a little fortress when needed. Nothing is getting through these stone walls.'

Gobkin nodded, but was too frightened to say

anything. Mum stroked his hair to reassure him.

'We need to face these Smidgens,' said Abel. 'Show them we are not going to be intimidated.'

'We need to *talk* to them,' said Gafferty. 'Show them that we're their friends. This is all a terrible misunderstanding, and fighting isn't going to solve anything.'

'They might not give us the chance,' said Abel. 'Wyn, I want you to get your wings on and fly back to the Roost. Tell the squadrons to come here immediately. And tell them to come armed. You too, Will.'

'I'm staying here, Uncle,' Will said defiantly. 'I want to find that Quigg and give her a piece of my mind.' *This adventure's changed Will*, thought Gafferty. *He's normally a worrier, not a warrior.*

'Whatever you're going to do, do it now,' said Mum, who had been keeping watch at the kitchen window. 'It won't be long before they find their way down here, if those sniffer-rats are any good at their job.'

Wyn turned to go, but paused and drew Gafferty to one side.

'I'm sorry I was so angry with you,' he said quietly. 'I'm just trying to look after Will. I get overprotective of him. He doesn't remember our parents, but I do, and I don't want to lose him too. I don't want him to lose you either.'

Gafferty didn't say anything, but just squeezed his hand.

He disappeared down the stairs. Gafferty, feeling a weight lift from her shoulders, ran to her room and threw on her clothes. She drew out the knife from her pocket. It sparkled as it always did, but tonight she felt especially comforted by its glow. She wasn't afraid to use it – she'd destroyed one of Claudia's ghosts with it already – but only to protect herself and her brother. To attack someone else, to attack another Smidgen, seemed very wrong. She couldn't do it and, somehow, the knife knew.

When she returned to the kitchen, Dad had his beetle leather coat on, and his round cap and goggles. He clearly meant business: he was carrying an Allen key club, and had been to the workshop to fetch a pencil-sharpener blade from the cat food tin that acted as a weapon store. Will also carried a stick. Gafferty wished hard that he wouldn't have to use it.

Mum kissed them all goodbye, even a surprised Uncle Abel.

'I'll never forgive any of you if you allow yourselves to get hurt,' she warned. 'And may the spirits help any Burrow Smidgen who attempts to get in here. I'm a match for your dad with the blunt end of a pencil, and if things get really bad, I can always set Grub on them!'

They left the House silently, Dad leading the way. Mum shut the door behind them; the sound of heavy rat-proof bars being put across it meant there was no turning back. They jogged through the cave and crept into the dark basement.

'I hope Wyn's got out in time,' whispered Will as they climbed up the pipe to the basement door. Gafferty suddenly seized his arm and pointed ahead of them.

'Is that Wyn crawling under the door?' she said. 'No, wait—'

Before anyone could stop her, she ran towards the figure, grabbing them by their boot.

'I've got you!' she said, dragging them backwards. 'You're my prisoner now, Burrow-bonce!' Quigg kicked out at her, but Gafferty held firm. 'We know what you've been up to, secretly leading an army of Burrow Smidgens here.'

They circled her so she couldn't escape. Gafferty let go of Quigg's foot. She sat on the floor and folded her arms sulkily.

'I was going to try and stop them,' she said. 'Yes, it's true – I did leave a scent trail for them to follow. I didn't mean for them to send an army. Just a couple of riders to scare you. I still didn't trust you after everything that happened with that daft Crumpet person. You arrived at the Burrow and then the Big Folk woman with her ghosts started digging us up right after that business with the Jewel. It was too much of a coincidence.' She sniffed miserably. 'But when I saw your family all together, and the trust you showed me in letting me stay, and the kindness ... well, I felt bad. You didn't seem like troublemakers, even if you're all daft and your dad is a grumpy bonehead.'

'Takes one to know one,' muttered Will, but Dad laughed.

'She's right enough,' he said.

'I hid when the bird folk arrived and again just now when I saw that other one leave,' Quigg continued.

'So Wyn got out all right,' said Will, relieved.

'What do we do now?' said Gafferty.

'It's too late to stop them coming to the factory,' said Quigg, 'but I've removed the scent threads that point the way down to your house, so the rats won't go down there.'

'But will they listen to you when they arrive?' said Abel. 'Will you be able to stop them?'

'Will you be able to stop the Roost Smidgens from attacking them?' countered Gafferty. 'They think they're coming to battle – that's what Wyn will tell them.'

Abel looked troubled. This could all go horribly wrong.

Then they heard a sound, a faint pattering and scratching of movement, furtive and stealthy, filtering through from the factory on the other side of the door.

'It's too late now,' said Quigg. 'They're here.'

26

The Battle of the Chocolate Factory

The five of them slid underneath the door. Although they could hear scurrying feet coming from somewhere in the factory, there was little to see in the gloom. The Big Folk workers always left some lights on at night to deter burglars, but they only shone dimly and gave the factory a distinctly spooky atmosphere. Shadows of the sweet-making machinery loomed over the Smidgens like misshapen, multi-limbed monsters. The darkened conveyor belts wound around the floor, gigantic serpents twisting in and out of pipes that reached up to the ceiling like the trunks of colossal, many-branched trees. To the Smidgens, they may as well have been navigating their way through a haunted fairytale forest.

'We left our wings up there, where we landed,' whispered Abel, pointing to the top of a pile of boxes. 'If Will and I take to the air we can try and monitor the movements of the rats below. We might be able to warn you of anything coming your way.'

'We're going to try talking to them first,' insisted Gafferty.

'It's always best to have a backup strategy,' said Dad. 'Rats are rats. One animal out of control could easily trample you into the ground, whether it means to or not.'

Will and his uncle made for the boxes while Gafferty, Dad and Quigg cautiously crept forwards, darting from one hiding place to another.

'There's only two entrances to the factory from the Tangle,' said Dad, as they stepped out from under a trolley. 'The mousehole over by the fudge-making machine is too small for a rat to go through, but the one in the storeroom could fit a rat. We'll head there and—'

They never heard his plan, as he was knocked flying by a large shape that flew out from behind a tank of food colouring, and which then scampered back under cover. Gafferty's heart went to her mouth as she saw her father tumbling across the ground, his Allen key clattering loudly as it fell from his hands. He came to a stop and, for a moment, lay still. Gafferty wanted to run to him but Quigg grabbed her arm, dragging her back to the shelter of the trolley. Dad groaned quietly, then slowly looked up towards them. He gave a shaky thumbs up – he wasn't hurt, just winded!

'That was a rat,' hissed Quigg. 'And there was someone riding it. Once they have your scent, they can follow you anywhere. We must find the Chief. It's the only way to stop this.'

'Chief Talpa,' Gafferty yelled. Despite being tiny, her voice echoed through the silent building. 'If you can hear me, answer me. It's Gafferty Sprout. Please can we talk?'

'We're not here to talk, child,' growled the reply from somewhere close. Too close for comfort. 'You brought destruction and desecration to our home. And now, you're holding one of our own as a prisoner. This is war!'

'No! I'm not a prisoner!' cried Quigg, but her voice was drowned out by the pitter-patter of

many feet and the yells of many voices. Suddenly the whole factory was filled with a terrifying, raucous noise. Arrows made from bramble thorns pinged off the floor around them.

'It's no good,' said Gafferty, trying to be heard over the commotion. 'We need to run!'

They fled from the trolley, dragging Dad to his feet from off the floor, and headed back towards the basement.

Then Dad stopped abruptly, grabbing Gafferty's hand.

'We mustn't lead them to the House,' he said. 'Think of Mum and the boys. We have to draw them away and escape.'

'The rats' sense of smell is too sensitive,' said Quigg bleakly. 'They're homing in on us. They'll find us eventually.'

'Not if they can't smell us,' said Gafferty, an idea forming. 'There's plenty of strong-smelling things in here.'

'Aniseed!' said Dad. Gafferty grinned, despite how scared she was.

'What's that?' said Quigg.

'The Big Folk use aniseed to flavour their gobstopper sweets,' Gafferty explained. 'The smell of that would overpower anyone. For a rat, it will be like trying to see through a fog.'

At that moment, something stirred the air over their heads, and Will's glider passed above them.

'Rats heading towards you!' he called, as an arrow shot past his ear. 'You need to move – now!'

They started running, heading in the direction of the flavourings department. Gafferty knew it was on the far side of a canyon of crates and machinery, having been on scavenging missions there several times before. The three Smidgens charged into the muddle of boxes, switching back and forth along its many twisting paths. Several times, rats jumped out at them, but Dad wasn't going to be surprised again.

'Look out!' he bellowed, as one of the creatures barrelled towards them. He swung his club and the creature swerved to avoid it, sending its rider sprawling to the ground, cursing furiously.

'We need help,' said Gafferty after they narrowly dodged another rat raider. 'Will!' she called, as the boy and his uncle made another pass over them. 'We need to get to the aniseed store – can you guide us to it? A rat-free path would be nice!'

'Keep going straight on!' he said. 'It's all clear to the syrup vat. Then go left.'

Abel flew off in another direction but reappeared moments later, a bag hanging from his glider.

'This should slow those rats down,' he shouted. 'Fudge, still soft from the cooking pot – and very sticky.' He darted about the factory, throwing dollops of it to the floor. Judging by the dismayed voices of the Burrow Smidgens, it was having an effect, and some of the rats may have even stopped to eat it. It didn't stop all of them, however, and the arrows continued to rain down, glancing dangerously off the surrounding walls of boxes.

'Isn't there a quicker way?' said Quigg, as they sheltered under a workbench.

Dad shook his head irritably but then his eyes suddenly lit up.

'The conveyor belt,' he said, pointing upwards. 'It runs from this bench past the flavouring store. It will get you there in no time. And over the heads of everyone else.'

'What about you?' said Gafferty.

'I'll have to stay by the control buttons, to make it stop at the right second. And you'll have to keep your wits about you, or you'll be in all sorts of trouble.'

'What trouble?' said Gafferty. It sounded like a great idea.

'Once the conveyor belt starts, the machinery it travels through starts as well. If you don't watch out, you'll be coated in chocolate, sprinkled with hazelnuts, chopped into chunks and wrapped up like a birthday present with a bow on top. A chocolate box with a nice selection of Smidgen pieces.'

'It's either that or being run over by a rat or shot by arrows,' said Quigg.

'Death by chocolate it is then,' said Gafferty.

27
What Next?

Using her pin hooks and fishing line, Gafferty clambered up the side of the conveyor belt. Dad followed, and then they both hauled the less nimble Quigg after them. Will and Abel kept the Burrow Smidgens distracted by swooping low and throwing fudge at them, making sure their arrows were pointed away from the helpless climbers.

'We could have sent your flying friends to get the aniseed,' said Quigg, who clearly wasn't used to this kind of exertion.

'They're more useful to us in the air,' said Dad. 'And it's safer for them too. No reason why more people should get hurt than necessary.' He ran to the control box next to the belt and sat on top of it, placing his hands on the start button. 'Are you ready?'

They nodded. He slammed his fists into the button. An alarm buzzed and a red light warned the belt was about to move. With a shudder it came to life, the sudden motion knocking the girls off their feet. They found themselves being carried on a winding rubber road, heading for the other side of the factory. Worryingly, machinery up ahead also began to whirr into action.

The noise and lights drew the attention of the rat riders below. A couple of riders pointed up at them, recognising Quigg. They spurred their rats towards the conveyor, and the animals bounded up the side, spanning the distance in a single jump. The two girls saw the danger and began to run along the wobbling conveyor belt as the rats chased after them.

'Gafferty!' called Dad. 'Hook yourself into the belt and hold on tight!'

'Why?' She looked around at him. The rats were gaining and would be upon them in seconds.

'Don't ask questions, you bother-brain – just do it!'

Gafferty knelt down on the belt, then took her pin hooks and sunk them into the soft rubber. She held one while Quigg hung on to the other. The rats had almost reached them, their beady eyes glaring, the shouts of the riders urging them on. She wanted to shut her eyes but found she couldn't, unable to resist the terrifying sight.

'Get ready!' yelled Dad.

The conveyor trundled towards a pillar, where it would make a sharp bend to the left. Dad waited for the right moment, then hit the stop button as hard as he could, just as they reached the turn. The sudden halt threw them forward, but the hooks kept them secure and stopped them from flying off the conveyor. The rat riders weren't so lucky. They were flung right off the belt, the squealing animals plummeting into piled sacks of sugar that lay below.

Dad restarted the conveyor with a laugh, but there were still dangers ahead.

'Chocolate coating coming up!' he warned.

The conveyor belt plunged through the dark opening of a machine. It was very warm inside. A cascade of melted chocolate poured down from above, glistening, rich and sickeningly sweet. They were swept through it, Quigg screaming with horror as she was drenched in the hot, sticky liquid.

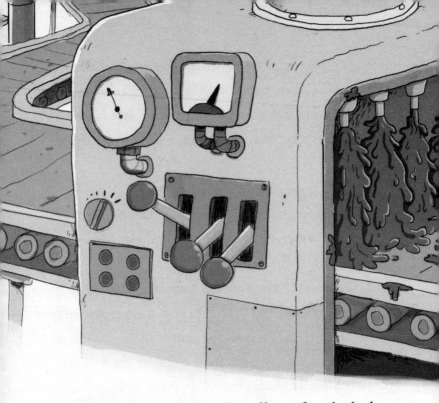

'That wasn't so bad!' said Gafferty after she had spat
out a mouthful of chocolate. 'But it's going to take ages to
wash this off!'

Quigg was about to speak when they were bombarded
by a shower of hard, sharp rocks.

'Ow!' Quigg cried. 'What's this?'

'Hazelnut chips!' said Gafferty, trying to shield herself
as the nut fragments rained down on them. 'Hang on –
we'll soon be out of it!'

They emerged from the other side of the machine,

bruised and hot. Quigg

pulled bits of hazelnut from her hair.

'I should have known this would be a ridiculous idea!'
she moaned.

'We're almost through,' said Gafferty. 'The aniseed store
is just beyond this machine. But it's the trickiest one yet.'

'Why?'

'It's the Giant Slicer. Get ready to move and move fast.
If you get it wrong by a Smidgenmetre you'll only be

needing one shoe or half a coat when you come out the other side.'

Quigg gulped, but it was too late to do anything else. The Great Slicer swallowed them up. Gafferty grabbed Quigg's hand as huge whirring steel blades swept down into their path. She'd have to do the thinking for both of them. This was all about reflexes and reaction times, skills she had been taught by Mum and Dad. Quigg didn't have this kind of experience. Escaping from tricky situations was what the Sprouts were good at. It was Rule Four, Gafferty's favourite rule, she realised. *If in doubt, make it up.* Sometimes it didn't work – but mostly it did, and that was enough.

'Go left! Now right! Right again!' Gafferty commanded, dragging Quigg from side to side as the cutters sliced past them, dodging their razor-sharp edges, and guiding them through on a clear, safe course.

Then, as soon as it had started it was over. They were out of the machine. Quigg could barely speak. She was shaking and whimpering.

'I lost my tail,' she said. The string mousetail from her coat had been sliced clean off.

'You're lucky that's all you lost,' said Gafferty. She waved at Dad, on the other side of the factory. She couldn't see the expression on his face but could imagine him trying to hide the fear. He waved back, then slammed his hands on the stop button. The conveyor belt bumped to a halt. Gafferty ran to its edge.

'There's the store,' she said. 'But I can see something that might be more useful.'

Quigg joined her. Gafferty pointed to a pile of plastic bags containing thousands of objects that looked like marbles.

'Aniseed gobstoppers,' she said. 'One of those bags could be the answer to our problem.' The bags were a short distance from the conveyor belt, but it was a long climb down to them. Will buzzed past.

'Are you OK?' he called. 'Uncle Abel says he can see the Roost flyers in the distance. But there's a swarm of riders heading towards you – you need to move!'

Gafferty could hear the noise of the army, moving like a river across the factory floor. It was now or never.

'I'm going to jump,' she said.

'What?' Quigg looked at her like she was mad. 'We're too high up! You'll never make it.'

'Yes, I will, with a run-up.' Gafferty took her knife out of her bag.

'I can't,' said Quigg, stepping away from the edge. 'I

can't do it. I'm scared. I'm not like you. You're too daft …
that is, I mean, too brave. I'm not as brave as you.'

Gafferty smiled kindly.

'It's fine. Stay here. The riders won't hurt you. You'll
be safe.'

She took a few steps back, then with a huge effort ran
with as much speed as she could to the edge of the belt
and launched herself into the air. She flew across the gap,
buffeted by the roar of the Burrow Smidgens below, their
arrows flying around her. She flung out her arm and
stabbed at the bag as she landed against it. The knife
sliced through the plastic as she plummeted downwards,
splitting open the bag and slowing her fall at the same
time. Hundreds of gobstoppers poured through the
opening, their pungent scent almost choking her as they
went by. They tumbled down on to the riders like
cannonballs, sending the rats squealing in all directions,
knocking or tripping over others. Riders were thrown to
the ground and found themselves chased through the
maze of machinery by the bouncing, rolling sweets.

Then the Roost Smidgens appeared through a skylight in the factory roof. Gafferty gasped at the sight as she finally stepped on to the ground, the gobstopper bag now empty. Like hundreds of birds, the flock of gliders flew in a formation led by Wyn, sweeping down from the ceiling and through the building, chasing the fleeing riders, who were terrified by the spectacle of the strange flying Smidgens, Smidgens with sticks and clubs. They herded the Burrow Smidgens back toward the Tangle entrance, where they were swallowed up by the dark mouth of the tunnel. The army was in retreat!

Gafferty looked back up at Quigg, who waved but suddenly started running. She was in a panic. What was she doing? Then Gafferty saw him: a lone rider, whose rat had clambered on to the conveyor belt. She watched in horror as the creature bore down on Quigg, the rider grabbing her by her chocolate-covered coat and dragging her off with him. Gafferty could do nothing as the rat jumped back on to the floor and followed the others, taking Quigg with it.

'Gafferty, love!' She was still staring after the escaping rats when Dad's arms wrapped around her, ignoring the mess of chocolate and hazelnuts. 'You were amazing! We did it, girl! We saw off those Burrow botherers all by ourselves. I'm so proud of you!'

Gafferty smiled, but she was smiling through tears.

'We're safe,' she said, sobbing into his chest. 'But what about Quigg? And what about Crumpeck and the Mirror? What do we do next? Smidgens fighting Smidgens. It's not all right. It's all a mess, Dad. A mess. And I caused it.'

Dad squeezed her tight.

'As for mess,' he said gently, looking around at the scattered sweets, 'there's one right here we need to clean up before the Big Folk come back to work. And then we'll talk. Then we'll sort all this out, you'll see. You're not alone, Gafferty. You've brought the Smidgens together, at least some of them, and we're going to need them all working together if we're to face whatever's coming next. Quigg knows we're on her side. Maybe she can spread the word to her clan. Maybe one day we will all be united. And when Smidgens are united, they can achieve great things. The greatest things, you'll see.'

Gafferty gave him a hug as chocolate dripped from her nose.

'Little people, big heart,' she whispered, and there was hope in her voice.

28
A New Tenant

Claudia slipped into the post office sorting room. If it had been creepy in daylight, it was positively sinister at night-time.

'You have news?' the client's voice rasped from the darkness.

'Better than that,' Claudia said, trying to hide her nerves. She reached into her handbag and pulled out a small wriggling creature.

'Kindly unhand me, madam!' Crumpeck said weakly. Claudia ignored him. She found a drawing pin and pinned Crumpeck by his coat to a noticeboard nearby. 'I must protest at this indignity!' he said, flapping his arms and legs about like an upturned tortoise.

'Is that all?' said the client.

'No.' There was a hint of triumph in Claudia's voice. She reached once more into the handbag and brought out the Great Jewel, which sparkled in the gloom. The client inhaled sharply.

'You've found a piece of the Mirror! Finally!'

'And we know that Gafferty Sprout has another piece. That just leaves the third.'

'Ah, I know where that is. I have remembered.' The client chuckled. 'And it's right under the Smidgens' noses.'

'Tell me,' said Claudia. 'I'll go and fetch it at once.'

'No,' said the client. 'I no longer have need of you. Our contract is terminated.'

'What? You can't do that!' Claudia was shocked. This was very irregular. She felt uneasy. Her instincts told her there was something else going on here. It began to feel like a trap.

'I *can* do that, and I have. However, I have someone here who is very keen to do business with you.'

From the shadows a figure stepped forward, his black eyes unblinking, his clammy bald head glistening. The figure smiled and licked his lips with his black tongue.

'Good evening, Claudia,' said Mr Ribbons. She gasped.

'What's the meaning of this?' she shrieked.

Ribbons just kept smiling hungrily. He moved slowly and deliberately towards her, saying words she didn't understand. Magic tingled over her skin. She didn't remember anything else after that.

Some time later, she woke. She found herself sitting inside ... what exactly? Smooth, transparent walls surrounding her. Windows on all sides. She was inside an object made of glass. Fear crept through her, a cold realisation. She glanced to either side. There were two other glass objects beside her, two faces staring back at her: Totherbligh and Hinchsniff. They looked at her curiously, almost pityingly. She was one of them. She was trapped inside a bottle. And that could only mean one thing: she was now a ghost ...

Acknowledgements

It's been a difficult couple of years for everyone, so I'd like to extend an extra special thank you to the editors, designers and Sales and Marketing folk at Bloomsbury for all their efforts to keep everything running during 2020–21. There have been tough times for booksellers, festival organisers and librarians too, but I'd like to thank them for their continued support of authors in some really exceptional circumstances. We're all very grateful! Thank you to Seb Burnett for once again putting his distinctive and hilarious mark on the world of the Smidgens with his brilliant illustrations. Finally, thank you so much to my departing editor, Lucy Mackay-Sim, who has been a patient, encouraging and inspiring guide through five books! I couldn't have done this without her and I wish her the very best in her new adventures.

Look out for
more adventures with

The SMiDGENS

COMING SOON!

Have you read all
THE DUNDOODLE
MYSTERIES?

AVAILABLE NOW